A SCOUT IS BRAVE

Jay Jordan Hawke

First Kindle Edition Published in July, 2010.
First Paperback Edition published in January, 2011.
Copyright © 2010 by Jay Jordan Hawke

All rights reserved.

Visit Jay Hawke on the web: http://www.jayhawke.weebly.com

ISBN-13: 978-1456426705
ISBN-10: 145642670

Dedication

For Steven Cozza who had the courage
to found "Scouting for All" at age 12.

For the countless gay teens who feel like
they are alone in this world.

For Matthew Shepard, who was brutally
beaten to death by an Eagle Scout.

And for Mom, of course.

Credits:

Cover designed by Jay Jordan Hawke

CHAPTER 1

Joshua Ishkoday awoke from a very sound sleep. A distant train whistle had wrestled him to consciousness. It was 5:00 a.m. Getting up this early didn't matter to Joshua. His radio alarm was set for 5:10 a.m. He almost always beat it. And besides Joshua had a busy day for which he had to prepare. The bus would be leaving at 8:00 a.m., and he didn't want to show up late. Josh wasn't exactly enthusiastic about his first day at camp, but he was hoping to make some friends. It wasn't easy being a new kid. Joshua couldn't wait for the nineties to be over. Adulthood will be so much easier, he thought.

Joshua slipped off his boxers and made his way to the shower. The shock from the ice cold water instantly jerked him to full consciousness. The added awareness made him realize how anxious he was about the day. Joshua had never been the new kid before.

Joshua got out of the shower and slowly dressed himself. He heard his radio go off in the background. Nirvana was playing, one of his favorite bands. "Smells Like Teen Spirit" seemed very appropriate today. Joshua couldn't help but hum along, as he packed his gear. Joshua stalled for a second, as he looked around for his Scout uniform. Where had he put it? It was brand new and very expensive, so naturally enough he couldn't find it. Joshua knew he should have packed the night before.

1

The song on the radio finished playing and was quickly replaced by a news report. Absorbed with finding his uniform, Joshua barely paid attention.

"The brutal murder of Matthew Shepard continues to captivate the nation, more after this quick announcement."

Joshua had no idea who Matthew Shepard was, but the murder must have been pretty brutal, he realized, to be making the national news. But Joshua didn't have time for the news. He had to find his uniform and finish packing.

"There you are," Josh mumbled, as he spotted his uniform hanging over his bathroom door. It looked clean and pressed. His mother had obviously suspended it there for him. Josh grabbed his uniform and shoved it carelessly into his backpack. He had camped out many times before, but he wasn't used to packing anything so formal.

The news story came back on. "Matthew Shepard, the young gay teen who was brutally murdered back in October..."

"Joshua, are you up?" his mother interrupted from outside his room.

Joshua zipped his backpack.

"Josh!" she yelled again, this time knocking on his door.

"Yes, Mom, I'm getting ready!" Joshua responded frustrated by the intrusion. He slammed the off button on his radio and rambunctiously opened the door.

"Oh, there you are," she said, stating the obvious. "I got breakfast ready."

To Joshua, it sounded more like a command than an offer, but it was hard to tell with his mother. He picked up his backpack, threw it over his shoulder, and headed off towards breakfast. It would be his last real food for at least a week. Josh was determined to enjoy his "last meal." As he ate, the

CHAPTER ONE

words on the radio he had just heard emerged from his mental buffer. "Young gay teen?" Joshua curiously mused. Had he heard that right?

*****

The bus ride had been long, but it would soon come to an end. Walls of pine and birch trees had finally replaced the monotonous open country, betraying the fact that camp was close at hand. Finally, Joshua had something else to stare at out the window other than country roads and cornfields.

The monotony had taken its toll on the other boys in the bus as well. The first couple of hours went fine. The boys who hadn't slept quietly passed the time reading or playing handheld video games. But such distractions could only last so long. As the hours passed, their attention spans decreased, and they desperately looked for something, anything, to occupy their short attention spans.

Joshua was overcome with relief as the bus entered a forested area, not only because it signified their immanent arrival at camp, but because this was his territory now. Ever since he was a little kid, the forests provided Joshua with a safe retreat from his unbearably rigid parents. His earliest memories were of a particular spot near a lake by his old house back on the reservation in northern Wisconsin. He would lean up against a white birch and gaze at the moving clouds reflected in the lake for hours. The sounds of loons and other singing birds merged with the smell of pine, alleviating any excess stress brought about by parental confrontations.

In this environment, Joshua often thought about his half Ojibwa heritage. His ancestors once occupied these woods prior to the arrival of Europeans. Joshua's parents kept him apart from the culture as much as possible, but he read about the Ojibwa whenever he got the chance. He felt a kinship with them. His ancestors revered the same kind of spiritual qualities in nature that drew Joshua to the forests.

While Joshua took great pride in his heritage, his parents discouraged it. Joshua was only part Indian, and his parents knew nothing of the culture from which they descended, even though his whole family grew up on the reservation. These days, more white people lived on the reservation than full-blooded Indians. Many of them owned land and houses on the lands once owned completely by the Ojibwa. A casino, camp grounds, and numerous arts and crafts shops catered to the tourists from Illinois, mostly Chicago, who overran the area in the summer. The only activity that betrayed a Native American influence were the frequent summer pow wows, which attracted relatively huge crowds, but again, mostly tourists. Joshua's parents, of course, prohibited Joshua from attending them. That didn't stop him from slipping in to one every now and then. He had become a rather proficient dancer.

While Joshua was only part Indian, he bore many of the stereotypical characteristics. His hair was long and dark, and his skin looked very tan. His eyes betrayed a hint of his ancestry. Joshua used to wear an earring with a feather worked into it, but his parents quickly put an end to that. Joshua next tried something even more obvious by tying a traditional head feather into his hair. That got him grounded for several weeks.

That didn't stop Joshua from learning what he could. Even with reservation activities being restricted for him, he had many sources of information. He could read books from the reservation library, he could talk with his teachers, or his preferred method, he could talk with the many elders that lived on the reservation. Joshua used to talk with his grandfather a lot about the Ojibwa, but his grandfather had passed away years ago.

Joshua's love for nature, however, he got on his own. The forests were prevalent on the reservation, providing the draw for so many summer tourists. Joshua came to life whenever he jogged through the forests surrounding his house. They offered him a convenient escape from the unbearable constraints of his upbringing, a place where he could discard the tension and anxiety he often felt around his parents. An awesome sense of freedom took hold in such moments.

Joshua couldn't discuss these feelings with his parents. They did not understand. Both of his parents were strict Protestants, having succumbed to the preachings of invasive reservation missionaries. Such was all too common on his reservation. There was a time when Ojibwa religion was severely sanctioned. At some point it simply became easier for people to be Christians. Joshua was never one to take it easy, and he ignored the preachers of "true religion," as they labeled it. Joshua got enough of that from his parents, and he wanted nothing more to do with it.

Joshua grew more withdrawn from his parents after their recent move to the big city of Rockford, Illinois. The city was small by most standards, but it was certainly large enough to contrast dramatically with reservation life in rural Wisconsin. Now, Joshua had neither friends nor forest. His mother did not want him hanging around the house all the time, and she became discouraged by his increasingly rebellious tendency to challenge her authority. Joshua wasn't exactly a "problem-child." A simple sarcastic remark directed against his mother or father every now and then typically satisfied him. But this was too much for both of his parents, who attempted to instill strict Protestant values in him, especially ones that stressed unquestioned obedience towards authority.

Joshua's parents usually reacted disproportionately to any incident with their son. "Mouthing off," no matter how innocuous, had to be dealt with. Usually his father would deliver a diatribe about respecting one's parents. The obligatory Biblical quotes always followed. Josh would then be grounded, but he usually didn't care. He quite effortlessly slipped out the window and disappeared into the forest. He sometimes even caught the latest pow-wow with some of his friends.

Joshua could no longer partake in such episodic freedoms now that he was in Illinois. With his only outlet gone, his patience with parental authority lessened. His parents quickly noticed. They became concerned that he was not developing into proper 14-year-old Christian boy. They would have been even more concerned had they realized that Joshua no longer considered himself a Christian.

Joshua's mother hit upon the perfect solution to her son's increasingly insufferable nature. He needed a good influence in his life. She learned from the minister at their new church about a local Boy Scout troop that the congregation sponsored. She figured the Boy Scouts would be the perfect way to instill proper Christian behavior and beliefs in her son, especially since the minister of the church was also the Scoutmaster for the troop. Joshua's parents trusted that Pastor Robert Natas, or simply Pastor Bob as he preferred to be called, was just the right man to instill these values in Joshua. They had only been in Pastor Bob's congregation for a month, but they got to know him pretty well. He was stern with the kids and knew how to properly discipline them. That was exactly what Joshua needed, according to his parents. The other kids in the troop would likewise exemplify proper Christian morality, unlike Joshua's old friends from back home. They were ill mannered and didn't seem to respect authority, according to Josh's parents. No doubt, his parents felt, these friends had influenced their son too much.

But the kids in Troop 24 had perfect credentials. They were Boy Scouts after all, Josh's mother reasoned. She recalled Pastor Bob's list of Scout qualities. He had stressed to her that all Scouts were taught to be "trustworthy, loyal, helpful, obedient, cheerful, thrifty, brave, clean, and reverent." Pastor Bob was a good salesman, but Joshua's mother only had to hear the "obedient" part before she was won over. This was just what her son needed at an age when peer-pressure was everything. The Boy Scouts of America would give their son a good Christian education.

*****

The bus pulled up into the camp parking lot. The three kids sitting behind Joshua on the bus slammed their Playboy magazines shut and quickly tried to shove them into their packs as Pastor Bob walked down the aisle to wake everyone up. One of the boys, Ken Fenton, immediately dropped his magazine on the floor in a rush to hide it from their fast approaching Scoutmaster.

"Fuck!" Ken shouted, as he frantically grabbed for the magazine and slipped it into his backpack before Pastor Bob had the chance to see the kind of quality literature the kids used to pass their time.

Joshua didn't know any of these people. He had only moved to Rockford in late May, and this was his first Scouting event. His parents enrolled him just in time for summer camp. Joshua was actually kind of excited about camp. He knew little about Boy Scouting, but he was happy to hear that the camp was only about an hour away from his reservation. Joshua was also happy to be getting away from his new home in Illinois.

But now Josh wasn't so sure about the camping trip. These kids weren't like his old friends on the reservation. They came across as unfriendly and cliquish. The boys made no attempt during the 6-hour bus ride to befriend Joshua. Even amongst themselves, they spent most of their time insulting each other. "Fag" or "queer" were always the insults of choice and seemed to be particularly offensive. The boys pretty much shrugged off any other insult.

Joshua had not yet given up on making friends. Perhaps he just sat by the wrong crowd. After all, the kids up front seemed much less threatening. Then again, they were also sitting close to Pastor Bob, who kept a stern eye on everyone around him in a relentless attempt at control. Joshua noticed that one boy in particular seemed to get a lot of Pastor Bob's attention. This boy sat right next to Pastor Bob. He had been rather quiet throughout the entire trip, no doubt afraid to do or say anything that Pastor Bob might consider inappropriate. Joshua felt sorry for this boy. He looked like he wanted to be anywhere else in the world right now.

There were other reasons that Joshua felt uncomfortable sitting near the back of the bus. The boys around him seemed rather obsessed with sex. Why did these kids so childishly

CHAPTER ONE

drool over their porn magazines? It was all they had talked about for several hours now, Joshua noted. His old friends were never this obsessed with sex. It was a subject that they never discussed. Josh wondered if his old friends avoided sex talk when he was around because they knew that Joshua was different. Joshua never actually told them he was gay, but his friends knew. Either way, his old friends didn't care. They grew up with Joshua, and they were all best friends.

But things were different now, Joshua sensed. These guys didn't seem the type to accept "faggots" and "queers," as they called them. Joshua knew that he would have to hide the fact that he was gay.

Pastor Bob made his way past Joshua, as he arrived to rouse the back of the bus. "Come on," he yelled, "wake up, we're here!" He grabbed one of the sleeping kids by the ear and pinched it hard.

"Now!" he yelled, "We don't have all day!" The boy jumped out of his seat and grabbed for his backpack. His ear hurt badly, but he wasn't about to let it show in front of the other kids.

Joshua stood up and reached for his pack. He had been reading the Boy Scout Handbook to familiarize himself with Scouting and had noticed a section on Native Americans. As Pastor Bob roamed up and down the aisles announcing their arrival at camp, Joshua started to put the book into his pack. One of the boys behind him saw the section he was reading and quickly questioned Josh's taste in literature.

"What the hell are you reading, Indian boy?"

Joshua was taken aback by the interest the boys suddenly showed in him. They had virtually ignored him for the entire trip. And besides, what was the big deal in reading a section

9

about Indians? Everyone in the Boy Scout troop was supposed to have read the Handbook. Josh didn't know how to respond.

He didn't have to. Before he had the chance, another boy joined in on the conversation. "Don't worry," he said with a wicked grin. "We'll show him some real reading material later," the boy avowed, no doubt referring to the Playboy that he had just shoved into his backpack. The other boys laughed.

Just great, Joshua thought. "What the hell have I gotten myself into?" he muttered quietly to himself. These Boy Scouts were a bunch of perverts. Joshua got up from his seat and made his way to the exit. Finally, Troop 24 had arrived at Camp Noitanimoba. It was going to be an interesting week.

CHAPTER 2

The bus pulled into the camp parking lot, and things immediately seemed unfamiliar to Joshua. Most noticeably, it was very hot, uncharacteristically so for northern Wisconsin. Joshua stepped off the bus and followed the other boys over to the side where Pastor Bob and the bus driver unloaded the gear. Mostly this involved throwing everyone's stuff on the ground and shouting, "Grab it!"

The bus sat at the edge of camp in a gravel-covered parking lot. It felt like a desert as the sun reflected off the gravel. But the forested area surrounding the parking lot was beautiful. Josh noted the characteristic scent of a nearby lake. He took a deep breath and let it out. All his tensions and anxieties seemed to vanish. Maybe, he thought, this wouldn't be so bad after all.

Several other buses dotted the parking lot. Boys from all over the region were arriving, unloading their gear, and walking with it up to the main path that led into main camp. Many boys went shirtless, desperately hoping to absorb any hint of a breeze. Others tortured themselves by wearing jeans and a T-shirt. Rarely, one could spot the occasional boy who was decked out in his full Scout uniform.

"Come on, snap to it!" yelled Pastor Bob, clearly agitated as he urged the last kids off the bus. He turned to the last of the boys, who were waiting by the bus for instructions. The Scouts knew what to do, of course, but none of them were about to do anything until they were told.

"Move it!" Pastor Bob yelled in a commanding tone. "Grab your gear and follow me!" Everyone reluctantly grabbed for their backpacks and following several moans, they set off to find their campsite.

Enthusiasm quickly replaced lethargy, as the boys left the sweltering temperatures of the camp parking lot. Most Scouts simply referred to it as "The Desert." The term quickly caught on, and the camp staff eventually got in on the joke by placing a sign designating it as such in the parking lot. It was soon official.

Although Joshua had a lot of gear, he found the walk quite easy. He was used to hiking, and his physical condition was perfect for this walk. Hiking directly in front of him was one of the boys who had sat in front of the bus near Pastor Bob. Josh figured the boy to be about 13-years-old, one year younger than himself. The boy was having a difficult time hauling all the weight of his backpack, and he stumbled every thirty seconds or so. But he always caught himself.

The boy breathed heavily and desperately tried to hide the fact that he needed help. But this pretense didn't last long. The path started on an upward incline and the boy lost balance on his next stumble. Laughter from the older boys in front followed as the boy crashed to the ground. He didn't seem hurt, but he was obviously humiliated.

"What a wuss!" said one of the boys, loud enough for everyone to hear.

Joshua bent down next to the fallen boy to offer assistance, but he knew that the boy was more embarrassed than hurt.

"Are you okay?" Joshua asked concerned.

"Yeah, I'm fine," the boy responded defensively.

Joshua extended his hand to help the boy up. Realizing that Joshua's intent was not to badger him, he dropped his tough-guy attitude, smiled, and extended his hand. Joshua grasped the boy's hand and pulled, and the boy was soon back on his feet.

"Let me help you with some of this," Joshua offered, as he walked around to the other side of the boy. Joshua unhitched the boy's sleeping bag from his backpack and held it in his one free hand. It wasn't very heavy, but it was bulky and just enough to keep a novice unstable. The boy seemed more than happy to give up the extra baggage, and the two began the hike once again.

"I'm Joshua," he said, introducing himself to the boy.

"I'm Cody," the boy responded. He hesitated, and then added, "Cody Natas."

"Pastor Bob's son?" Joshua inquired.

"Yes, well, don't hold it against me," Cody said with a smile. Joshua snickered as they proceeded up the trail.

Cody hiked much more effortlessly now. He was grateful for Joshua's assistance, and Joshua was glad to have met a friend, even if it was the Scoutmaster's son. The trail continued upward for another couple of minutes. Joshua could have done the hike much more quickly by himself, but he tempered his pace so his new friend could keep up.

After only ten minutes in camp, Joshua had solved two problems. One, he had a friend; two, he had a tentmate. Cody had intended to tent with his father, but not by choice. It simply wouldn't look good to his other friends if he bunked with his father. It would reinforce his special status as the Scoutmaster's son, a position of authority and something to avoid if one wanted friends. Cody was thus relieved to discover that Joshua needed a tentmate.

It didn't take long for everyone to arrive at the campsite, as it was only about a ten-minute hike. The boys would have to take the same trail several times a day back to main camp where all the programs took place. But without all their gear to haul, the hike wouldn't be a problem, at least, not until it was time to leave at the end of the week.

Joshua liked their assigned campsite. Since they had left "The Desert," the heat didn't seem to be much of a problem anymore. Their site was well shaded from the birches and pines that ruled their surroundings. Sunbeams crept through the trees in intermittent spots, creating beautiful silhouettes on the foliage below. This was the Wisconsin that Joshua knew.

It didn't take long for Josh and Cody to set up their tent. The two boys had both done this many times before, and they worked well together. The tents were not huge. One couldn't even stand up inside without bending over. But they were good enough for sleeping in, and that's all they were meant for. Changing clothes proved a slight problem for those new kids unaccustomed to four-foot ceilings. But campers soon learned how to get dressed in a small space.

The boys were instructed to get into their swim suits as soon as their tents were up, so they could go down to the lakefront and take their swim tests. The lakefront was the center of many of the activities that would be happening during the week. Several of the camps' most popular merit badges were held there, including Swimming and Canoeing. There were also plenty of periods set aside for "free swim," where the Scouts could engage in unstructured fun. But before any of the boys could swim, the lifeguards on camp staff had to test each Scout to determine his strength as a swimmer. Stronger swimmers could take advantage of all the opportunities offered by the lakefront. Weaker swimmers were restricted to the shallow areas and, of course, became the subjects of many jokes.

Cody quickly tore his shirt off and threw it to the corner of the tent. This was the easy part of the ritual of "tent-dressing." The more difficult part was taking off one's pants. First year Scouts usually took their pants off while standing on their knees. This seemed the most natural way to do it, since most people undressed while standing up. However, a small tent offered no such luxury. There was no room to stand up in the common pup tents that Pastor Bob had purchased for the troop. The younger Scouts did the next best thing to standing up by undressing while standing on their knees. Cody had been in tents many times before. He had long since mastered tent dressing, and so he knew such methods were doomed to failure. He quickly lay on his back and yanked his pants off, demonstrating the proper way to do it.

Joshua liked to be a little more organized and was thus slower in getting undressed. He was still getting his swimsuit and towel out from his backpack, while Cody, now completely naked, just started to look for his suit.

Joshua glanced momentarily at Cody through the corner of his eyes. Cody had firm stomach muscles, and his broad shoulders and arm muscles showed him to be in much better condition than his performance on the hiking trail indicated. Josh caught himself staring, and quickly shifted his focus back to the task at hand. The last thing he needed right now was for his new friend to catch him with wandering eyes. Josh was much more shy about getting undressed in front of people, even though he was a year older than Cody.

Josh was too secure with himself to deny that he found Cody attractive. He could have suppressed these feelings and pretended to be attracted to girls, but it was no use. Joshua was gay, and he knew it. He also knew that no one could find out. Even with his friends back home, friends who would have accepted him, Joshua could not divulge his secret. He knew how society felt about gay people; he knew all the jokes and derogatory words. But this isn't what mattered to Joshua.

What mattered were the beliefs of his parents. He had seen the reaction of his father whenever homosexuality was brought up on TV or in conversations. "Damn gays trying to push their lifestyle on everyone," he often overheard his father complaining. His mother always followed up with an approving nod. Joshua remembered once his mother talking about a place where gays could be cured. Josh had no doubt that if his parents ever found out that their son was gay, he would end up at some such facility. The thought horrified him. It sounded medieval.

Cody finished slipping his swim trunks on and draped his towel around his neck, totally oblivious to the fact that he had an admirer. He then put his shoes on and slipped outside the tent. "Hurry up," he teased Joshua on the way out.

Joshua had the tent all to himself.

"Be right there," Josh shouted back. But he waited until Cody left before taking off the rest of his clothes.

*****

The lake was a remarkably refreshing sight. The water was a cool, light blue, perfectly reflecting the cloud free sky. One could see a line of pine trees in the distance, betraying the long width of the lake. The swimming area consisted of a small sandy spot cleared of trees and brush, but more than large enough to accommodate one hundred or so hot campers. This was "The Beach," as indicated by the signpost.

Joshua and his troop had a lot of waiting to do by the time they arrived at the beach, as many other troops had already arrived to take their swim tests. While Pastor Bob's troop waited, the camp medic went over each Scout's medical forms to see if anyone had a condition that would prevent them from swimming.

Joshua waited in line behind Cody. Further behind them stood Levi Nomed. Joshua recognized Levi immediately as the boy who questioned his taste in literature back on the bus. Joshua learned by now that most of the kids in the troop were pretty nice kids. Levi and his small gang of hooligans were the exception.

Levi and his gang were busy whipping each other with their towels and laughing whenever one of them got hurt. Levi's tall and slender body gave him an advantage not available to the smaller kids. Of course, Levi had other advantages as well. Levi was fierce, wild, and cold in everything that he did. He was unpredictable, often displaying a wild energy. One concentrated look from his eyes and everyone immediately backed down. Something in him commanded subservience. He was ruthless and menacing, and no one at camp wanted to mess with him. Levi's friends only hung with him because they were scared not to. Better to have someone like Levi on one's side, they reasoned, than to be the victim of his malicious nature. Levi's friends, however, weren't exactly innocent. They did enjoy Levi's special brand of amusement even if he sometimes took it too far.

Josh didn't feel intimidated by Levi and his mob anymore. He had yet to experience anything other than a little annoyance with them. Sure they were immature, but for now, at least, they seemed to be staying to themselves.

"Josh," Cody called, trying to get his new friend's attention.

Joshua immediately turned his interest from Levi and his gang of friends back towards Cody.

"Ouch!" one of Levi's gang members yelped after receiving a powerful slash to his side courtesy of Levi. A vibrant grin exploded across Levi's face.

"Pretty friendly guys, aren't they?" Cody said sarcastically.

"Yeah," Joshua agreed. "Why do they come to camp anyway? All they do is bully each other."

"They get in trouble everywhere," Cody responded. "Their parents send them to camp to keep them out of trouble at home. You know, let someone else worry about them for a week. That sorta thing."

Joshua decided not to let Levi's "fun" ruin his own attitude. Levi's gang could have their fun, and Josh and friends could do likewise. The two groups need not interact with each other. Camp appeared large enough to accommodate everyone.

The afternoon dragged on, and the heat became unbearable as they endlessly waited in line. The wait was long and tedious, and everyone just wanted to get in the water and get the swim test over with. Towel fights occupied Levi and his gang only so long, and soon their attention shifted to the younger Scouts around them.

Robert Enola, a small 11-year-old camper, had the misfortune of being at the end of the line, directly behind Levi and his gang. He would be the hapless victim of their boredom. Some of the younger Scouts could already understood this by the unfortunate position Robby occupied. Robby was not only the closest to Levi's gang, but he was the furthest from Pastor Bob, who stood at the front of the line. All the essential ingredients presented themselves to Levi: proximity, lack of oversight, and lots of boredom. Now all Levi needed was some sort of excuse, something to mix the ingredients and bring everything together.

Like Joshua, Robby was new to the troop. Unlike Joshua, however, Robby had yet to make any friends. He had talked to no one since they arrived at camp. His position in the back of the line made him a perfect target, but even more so, he had no friends, no protectors, and no one to care.

"What the fuck are you looking at?" Levi challenged Robby, beginning his favorite sport. The other kids in Levi's band immediately took interest in the challenge. They put their towels to rest and quickly joined in on the fun, happy to allow their own towel wounds some time to heal.

Levi's abrupt challenge surprised Robby, catching him off guard. Robby had just been standing alone minding his own business, lost in his own thoughts. Mainly he was trying not to look like a dork standing there by himself. He simply wanted to blend in with the crowd. Levi was not going to allow this. Robby found some solace in the hope that Levi was talking to someone else. That comfort only lasted a second.

"Answer me, you little fuck!" Levi challenged again, staring right into Robby's eyes.

"Excuse me?" Robby murmured, snapping out of his daydream. His voice cracked, and his eyes refused to meet Levi's wild and powerful stare. His heart immediately started to pound.

"I said, what the fuck are you looking at?" Levi shot back threateningly, this time shoving Robby back. The gang laughed riotously, almost as if on cue. The sight of this lonely and defenseless boy, totally powerless and totally unable to defend himself, was just too funny for these kids to bear.

"I'm not la- look- looking at...I'm, nothing," Robby said, desperately trying not to stutter. His cracking voice once again betrayed his fear. Sweat started dripping down his forehead. Any casual observer, unaware of what was happening, would have attributed the sweat to the heat. But none of the other kids were sweating. Robby prayed that his response, however pathetic, would be enough to get the gang to shift their attention elsewhere. Simultaneously, his mind frantically raced for a better answer. But he was terrified and his mind shut down. "Nothing," was all that Robby could deliver.

Prior to this confrontation, Robby had been lost in thought, reflecting on the day before him and how he had come to be at camp. Unlike Joshua, Robby was not completely new to the troop. He had been there for several months, pushed into the troop by caring, but naïve parents, who wanted Robby to make some friends.

But Robby was shy and quiet and didn't make friends so easily. He had no one at school to talk to, and his parents figured that the Scouts were a perfect place for him to get the necessary self-esteem required to let him shine. But Robby would come home from troop meetings each week begging his parents not to make him go back. They always inquired as to why, but that was a question Robby didn't know how to answer. Instead he always gave in and did as he was told. It was easier than articulating a weakness he barely understood. So when Levi asked Robby what he was looking at, Robby had no answer. He hadn't been looking at anything; he was daydreaming. Something Robby spent most of his time doing.

Levi, of course, could see that Robby was afraid and no threat to anyone. But fear was exactly what the boys were after, especially Levi. The boys seemed to feed off of it. Nothing Robby could have said would have offered him a reprieve. As long as the boys detected fear, their little game would continue. Levi had chosen his target well, and the fun was just beginning. Robby stood out helplessly, and nothing he could do would return him to the pleasant state of blending in. Levi simply would not allow that.

"Are you saying I'm nothing?" Levi accused angrily, purposely twisting the helpless boy's words. It was all part of the game, and Levi played it well.

"No, I didn't ma- mea- mean it that way," Robby stuttered apologetically. He frantically analyzed the situation in his head as he attempted to figure out what he had done wrong. Perhaps he had done something to offend Levi? But he hadn't done anything to anyone since he arrived.

Levi was delighted to hear Robby stutter. This was an added benefit that he hadn't anticipated when he chose his target. Levi always looked for someone weak and pitiful, but Robby was also different, a difference clearly present for all to hear with every word, with every cry.

Levi, of course, knew that Robby had done nothing to offend him. That's what provided the maximum quantity of delight. One simply used the victim's words against him in order to justify further attack. The idea was to make it look as if the victim was responsible for the hostilities. Bullies thrived on this kind of psychological torture.

Robby didn't know what else to say. He wanted to believe he could talk his way out of this. But he quickly realized that nothing he said would stop Levi. A single tear began to well up in his eye as he realized the helplessness of his situation.

"I'm sor- soor sorry," Robby finally squealed. "It was ja- ju- just an expression. I didn't mean an- anything by it." Robby cursed at himself for stuttering. "What's wrong with me?" he angrily chided himself. With that reflection, Levi had won completely. Robby had internalized the bullying, and from them on, he was lost

"Do you think I'm st- stu- stupid!" Levi said, mimicking Robby's stutter. He lunged forward and shoved Robby again. "Answer me you little shit!" Levi shouted furiously. "Answer me!"

Robby felt as if he was about to burst into tears, a sensation that only added to his mental and emotional torment. If he started crying, everything would be ruined for him. No one would hang around such a loser. In the twisted social fabric that governed adolescent friendships, crying was taboo. Robby would be a marked man and forever remain a target for bullies like Levi. Robby knew all of this and did everything he could to hold back the tears. But the more he held back, the stronger the urge to cry became.

Joshua and Cody had been observing the situation, as was almost everyone else near the back of the line. Joshua had never seen anything like this before. He had grown up in a rural area where everyone had known each other since they were born. His friends got into fights, but they never purposely tried to humiliate each other for sheer amusement. This world was totally alien to Joshua. How could they pick on this totally defenseless kid? Why didn't anyone do anything about it?

CHAPTER TWO

Joshua couldn't just stand by and watch; he had to do something. It never occurred to him what he would be getting himself into. He never challenged a bully before.

Robby frantically held back his tears as Levi kept at him. But he was about to break. Levi was shocked that Robby hadn't started crying yet. But, Levi wasn't about to give up; he was having too much fun. His gang was excited and appreciative of the wonderful entertainment their leader had provided them. The gang had chosen Levi as their leader for a reason. He could always find ways to amuse them. Additionally, Levi's game was participatory, and his gang played their parts well. They pretended to sniff and cry, mercilessly mimicking the behavior that they anticipated from Robby.

"What's the matter Robby? Gonna cry?" Levi taunted, sensing that Robby was finally about to crack. It wasn't original, but it always worked.

"Leave him the fuck alone!"

A devastating silence followed. Robby stood in shock as his mind completely froze. Had his prayers been answered? Just when he was about to break out into tears in front of everyone, someone had actually ceased the spotlight for themselves. It was no longer a gang of five terrifying bullies against one helpless kid. Now the gang had someone else to play with.

Robby had no idea who had come to his defense. It didn't matter. What mattered was that everyone's attention had shifted. It was someone else's turn to experience the torture and humiliation of the spotlight. Robby had played the part long enough. At the same time, Robby felt horribly guilty for entertaining such thoughts. The last thing he wanted was for this other boy to be tortured in his place. After all, this boy had the courage to stand up to his tormentors. But it was out of

23

Robby's hands now. He couldn't even defend himself, let alone someone else. All he could do was revel in his new fortune, however brief.

"What are you doing?" Cody frantically whispered into Joshua's ear. Cody had also been watching the gang pick on Robby. But he had been around long enough to understand the hierarchy. One did not challenge bullies. They were older, stronger, and most importantly, they had greater numbers. He felt sorry for Robby, but there was nothing that could be done. The only thing to do was let the gang have their fun until they tired. But Joshua didn't seem to understand any of this. Joshua wasn't about to let them continue harassing this defenseless kid.

Cody didn't repeat his warning to Joshua. It was too late for that. Levi had already discovered that the challenge had stemmed from Joshua. Cody stepped back, instinctively distancing himself from Joshua and the huge spotlight that now marked him. He wanted to call for his father, but he knew that would only make things worse in the long run.

"Did you say something?" Levi inquired, not quite sure yet if this new kid was worth the effort.

"Just leave him alone," Joshua responded, lowering his tone a bit so as not to appear confrontational.

"Hey, it's Indian Boy from the bus," one of the boys from the gang informed Levi.

"Oh yeah," Levi said, recognizing Joshua. "So Indian Boy, did I do something to bother you? Am I picking on your boyfriend?" Levi stepped forward threateningly toward Joshua. His eyes fixed on Joshua's eyes, never wavering. They seemed to penetrate his psyche, analyzing his emotions, especially his fears, for any sign of weakness. Joshua had never experienced anything like this.

CHAPTER TWO

Cody tensed up. This was not good. His tentmate was now a target for humiliation. He did not want to get caught in the line of fire. What if the gang declared Cody a target by association? As with Robby, Cody felt some pangs of guilt for entertaining such thoughts. He tried to put them out of his head, but they were still there.

Robby and Cody expected to see Joshua cower as Levi approached him. At the very least, they thought he'd avert his eyes. But, he didn't. He caught Levi's gaze and never flinched.

Levi shoved Joshua forward just as he had done with Robby. That should have been the end of it. Levi had asserted his authority, and no one ever challenged it. Levi's gang took their cue and began their taunts, this time aiming them at Joshua.

"What's the matter, Squaw?" Levi asked. "Did we hurt your little boy friend?" He added the obligatory taunt, "Gonna cry now?"

Joshua did not cry or cower. He wasn't even the least bit afraid. Unlike Robby, Joshua only got angrier as Levi began to taunt him. Then to everyone's surprise, Joshua pushed Levi back, and he pushed him back hard. Levi's body smashed against the wood fence separating the lakefront from main camp. Levi was shirtless and screeched in pain as several splinters from the fence tore into his flesh. Blood rushed out, and Levi appeared to cry.

Joshua was a bit shocked by his own actions. He never felt this angry before and acted without thinking. He didn't realize how hard he had pushed Levi and was surprised how easily Levi flew back. Levi's fierce manner had evoked an apparent imperviousness. Yet, a simple push sent him flying. Joshua would never forget that.

The crowd was astonished at what they had just witnessed. It was nothing short of miraculous. A victim had fought back and apparently won!

This certainly took the fun out of things for Levi. His friends suddenly acted like they weren't paying attention to what was happening. Levi's legitimacy as leader had clearly been challenged. He would have to accept the challenge, or his friends would lose all respect for him. He slowly stood up and wrapped his arm around his back, rubbing his wound. A tear dripped off his face. Levi then saw the blood on his hand, and his eyes filled with rage. He approached Joshua, who stood his ground. None of the boys knew what was going to happen next. They had already witnessed impossible events and gave up trying to predict them. They had stopped their taunts; now they simply watched.

Pastor Bob had been paying attention to the swim tests, but as he looked back, he noticed the last half of his troop concentrating their attention on two boys staring intently at each other. He knew that something dire had replaced the innocent towel fighting. Pastor Bob had seen kids fight before. Personally, he had no qualms about letting kids fight things out without intervention. It built character, he felt. But this sort of fight would probably arouse too much attention. Pastor Bob obsessed over his reputation at camp, and there were plenty of other troops and Scoutmasters present. The last thing Pastor Bob needed was for his peers to think that he could not control his boys. This had to be stopped.

"You two! End it now!" he shouted in the direction of the scuffle, not even sure exactly who was involved.

An overpowering sense of relief struck both Robby and Cody. The spotlight faded. Adults had taken notice, and the incident would stop, for now, at least. Joshua also thought it had ended. He broke off his gaze and got back in line with Cody. Levi looked over to Pastor Bob and saw the futility of continuing his taunts. Pastor Bob met Levi's gaze and waited for his move. There was nothing Levi could do. He had lost. Levi reluctantly returned to his place in the line, while holding back the urge to rub his back. He couldn't show any pain, not now.

Pastor Bob felt good about his handling of the situation and for a second was glad it happened. It made him look good. He demonstrated true leadership. He saw an explosive situation and had taken charge. He beamed with pride as he turned his attention back to the swim tests.

"That was crazy," Cody whispered to Joshua, as the two stood in line once again waiting for their turn in the water.

Joshua didn't expect Cody's critical response. He had been too caught up in the fight to notice Cody's apparent disapproval. It never occurred to Joshua that he had behaved improperly in any way. His mind raced to explore where he went wrong. But he came up empty.

"I was just helping out that kid," Joshua explained, sounding a bit defensive. "He seemed to need it," he added, his tone bordering on sarcasm.

Cody said nothing in return. His conscience wouldn't let him. Joshua did the right thing, and deep inside, Cody admired Joshua's courage. But Cody also knew that they had a long week in front of them and despite some initial luck, Levi would not let things drop. Camp was a big place, which made it easy to avoid confrontations. But it also made it easy to avoid adults. Levi would be counting on that.

*****

Most of the Scouts in Pastor Bob's troop forgot about the incident before long. The swim test had cooled off all the boys, and for now, at least, Levi's temper seemed quenched. Just in case, however, Joshua stayed behind after completing his test to keep an eye on Robby. The test required that each boy swim one hundred yards, but the lifeguards only allowed two boys in the water at a time, so it took awhile to get through Pastor Bob's entire troop.

Since Robby was at the back of the line, he was the last to take the test. Pastor Bob, along with most of the troop, had already headed back to camp. No one remained to cheer for Robby when he finished. Joshua decided to wait for him. Besides, he wanted to insure that Levi didn't take advantage of Pastor Bob's absence.

Cody stayed behind with Josh. He knew now that he was crazy for associating with Joshua, but he also knew that he liked him. Josh's courage impressed him. It never really occurred to Cody that one could stand up to Levi. How could it possibly work? Yet Joshua stood before him as living proof that it could work.

Robby pulled himself out of the water and onto the dock, seemingly exhausted from his swimming test. Water dripped from his drenched, light brown hair, and he panted heavily as he made his way off the dock. He didn't realize anyone had been waiting for him. He even half expected that the lifeguards had left by now. He was surprised when he heard applause directed towards him, followed by shouts. "Good job, Robby!" he heard the voices cry out. "Congratulations!"

CHAPTER TWO

Robby was terrified. He thought the voices came from Levi and his gang, and that they were beginning the taunting all over again. Robby felt even more defenseless than before. He was exhausted and could barely move.

Robby gazed up from the water and saw Joshua and Cody smiling and cheering. It still didn't register with him that it was safe. Instinctively, he ignored them, suspecting for a second that it was some sort of set up. But his mind quickly pushed aside his deeply ingrained defense mechanisms as he finally noticed that the cheers were coming from the boys who had just saved his life.

Robby could barely walk after his exhausting swim. He stumbled as he made his way towards the lakefront fence exit where the two boys waited for him. "Way to go Robby!" the boys repeated. Robby smiled. For the first time since he arrived at camp, he had friends. And for the first time, he felt good about himself.

Robby grabbed his towel and made his way to Joshua and Cody. He covered himself with his towel and headed for the boys. A smile replaced his more typical stoic look. The sensation was unfamiliar to him, and he didn't know how to react. He tried to suppress his smile but couldn't. It bubbled upward, just like his earlier urge to cry had, but this urge he couldn't suppress. It seemed much more powerful. Perhaps it was stronger because it had been missing for so long. Still smiling, he simply said nothing.

Cody patted him on the back and repeated, "Nice job."

"Thanks," Robby said happily, almost crying once again. This time, it was from happiness.

"Pastor Bob gave us all free time before dinner," Joshua said to Robby, "and Cody and I are going to hike around camp and explore a bit. You can join us if you want." They hardly expected a negative answer. They both knew quite well that Robby would join them. It was either that or return to the campsite where Levi and his gang dwelt. Joshua and Cody started walking backwards, while still facing Robby, who lingered behind.

"Yeah, come along," Cody prodded. Robby quickly ran after them like a lost puppy dog. Once he caught up to them, they headed for a trail leading into the woods. They both put their arms on Robby's shoulder and quickened their pace.

The trail rose upward and winded around the lake. Steep bluffs led down from the trail to the lake below. The trail was mostly dirt held tightly together by roots from all the foliage covering the sides of the hills. Across the lake from their position, Joshua could see a rocky cliff about thirty feet high. It would probably take about twenty minutes to get over there at a normal pace, but they were not walking at a normal pace. They had two hours to kill before dinner, and Joshua was filling the time by taking his two new friends on a nature hike. Joshua's head was filled with all kinds of practical information about the ecology of this area. Cody and Robby looked around and saw only trees. Yet Josh could always identify the tree and often give a long lesson on how the Native Americans used it for canoes, or food, or whatever.

Joshua always threw a heavy dose of Indian Lore into his lectures. He had learned a lot from both books and from his grandfather and was surprised at how easily his lessons came back to him. He told his friends that Indians believed animals communicated with and taught people and that everyone had a spirit animal.

"What's a spirit animal?" Robby asked, mystified by Josh's heritage.

"It's sort of a helper. Each animal has its own special and unique power, and you can ask for help from the animal whose power you need the most." A nearby bird started chirping, and Josh immediately identified it to the other boys as a cardinal.

"Neat," Robby said. "What power do they have?"

"Courage," Josh responded.

Suddenly, the boys spotted the bird overhead, as is darted off. A red feather fell from the sky, floating gently to the ground and landing next to Joshua. Robby and Cody were mystified. Cody walked over to Joshua and picked up the feather. He stepped behind Joshua and stuck the feather in Josh's dark black hair. Cody struggled a bit to tie it in, but it stayed.

"Red Feather," Cody proclaimed. "That's what we'll call you."

Robby agreed. The name seemed to fit him perfectly. In Robby's eyes, no one exemplified courage more than Joshua.

Joshua liked his new name. It connected him to a tradition to which he was very close. Joshua smiled and the three boys continued on their hike.

The path reached a fork as part of the trail continued to bank around the lake. They took this trail, avoiding the other one that led back to main camp. Cody had been to this camp many times, and so he knew all the twists and turns quite well. The trail headed down towards the lake, and they entered a small clearing about twenty feet wide. The ground was filled with small plants and stones. At the end of the clearing was the lake. The sun didn't seem as menacing now as it began its late afternoon decent. Joshua figured it was about 4:30 p.m. The rocky cliff was closer now and appeared more majestic as the sunlight glared off its side.

"What is that?" Joshua asked Cody in awe of the cliff's beauty.

"That's Tommy Drapos' Point," Cody answered.

"Who is Tommy?" Robby asked, wondering why a point was named after him.

"Some kid, a former camper here, who supposedly fell off it many years ago," Cody explained. The cliff was named after him. They'll tell everyone the story at the campfire program tonight."

"When is the campfire?" Robby jumped in excitedly.

"About 8:30 p.m. tonight," Cody answered. "We have a while yet."

"Let's hike down there," Joshua said, pointing to Tommy's Point.

"We're not supposed to," Cody said obediently. "It's off limits to campers," he scolded, suddenly tensing up and taking on a serious and rigid tone. Cody realized he had been a bit harsh and softened his pitch. "Like I said, they'll explain it all tonight."

Robby was satisfied with Cody's answer, but Joshua couldn't break his gaze off away from the cliff. He felt compelled to go there, but he didn't know why. The sound of Cody and Robby laughing and shouting finally diverted his attention from the cliff. The two boys had fallen into a game of knee tag. The object was simply to tag the other person's knees. A player, however, could not shield his own knees. He could only block the other person's hands with his own. Robby was no match for Cody, who was taller and swifter. Every time Robby would go for Cody's knees, Cody would block and return the move, getting Robby every time. Robby didn't care. It was still fun.

Joshua soon joined in and gave Cody more of a challenge. Robby sat out and watched the two boys in mock battle. They walked around in a circle facing each other like two wrestlers. Robby laughed as they swapped at each other's knees, both blocking and failing to hit their targets. Finally, they called it a tie, and Cody patted Joshua on the back.

"Come on," he said, "We better get back to camp. It's almost time for dinner, and we've got a bit of a hike back."

"Okay," Joshua responded, panting a little. They were both tired from the game. Joshua felt surprised when Cody touched him on the back. It felt good deep inside. Even though he had only known Cody for a few hours, he felt something special towards him that he had never felt before.

Even though Joshua and Cody were worn out from the game, Robby still lagged behind the two on the way back. Joshua and Cody talked loudly so Robby would not feel left out.

As they reached their campsite, all the Scouts in their troop seemed to be doing their own thing. One group of boys sat around a campfire they had made and were busily telling jokes. Pastor Bob was in his tent taking a nap before dinner. Levi and his miscreants were at a picnic table playing cards and minding their own business. Cody worried that the gang might harass them some more, but the group simply ignored them. They seemed intent on their game.

"We're going back to our tent to get ready for dinner," Cody said to Robby. "Put your uniform on, and we'll walk down together." All the Scouts had to wear their Scout uniforms for dinner. The uniforms were hot, but that didn't matter to Pastor Bob. He insisted that everyone look their best for dinner.

Robby was relieved at the invitation. Even though he felt comfortable around his new friends, he was still too insecure to ask to sit with them at dinner. He had been terrified at the thought of having to sit alone. But that fear ended with Cody's invitation, and Robby ran excitedly back to his tent to change.

The joy on his face quickly transformed to fear as he approached his tent. It had been knocked over, apparently on purpose. Normally he would have just thought it fell over. Maybe he hadn't put the stakes in deep enough? But, Robby knew how to put up a tent, and this clearly hadn't fallen down by itself. With Levi and friends laughing nearby to themselves just loud enough for Robby to hear, Robby knew they had done it.

"Maybe you should learn to put up a tent," Levi yelled over to Robby. Levi's band laughed. One of them began to mimic crying sounds again, before another in the gang punched him on the arm as a reminder that they were playing a new game now.

Joshua and Cody overheard the laughter and looked toward Robby and his tent. They knew right away what had happened. Joshua reacted immediately.

"Hey Robby!" Joshua shouted. "Now that you got your tent down, it won't take you as long to move in with us!"

With that, Josh managed to turn Levi's little joke against him. Robby smiled back at Joshua and excitedly entered his fallen tent. Joshua and Cody laughed as they watched Robby collect his stuff. He crawled into his tent, and a little lump of canvas appeared and squiggled around a bit. Robby then emerged from his downed tent seconds later. He had his gear and ran toward Joshua and Cody, who were still waiting for him. Joshua's eyes caught the image of the Batmobile on Robby's sleeping bag as he approached. Joshua began to giggle. Cody joined in. By now, Robby could distinguish the mocking laughter of Levi and his gang from the playful taunts of his own friends.

"So, I like Batman," Robby said. "You gotta problem with that?"

"No problem," Joshua responded. "To the Bat-tent," he added, as they followed behind Robby. Unknowingly Robby had now earned his own nickname. They called him "Robin" from that point on.

Levi stared at them furiously as the three entered the tent. He had been beaten again, and keeping score had become an obsession for him. But it was only the beginning of the week, and Levi knew he had plenty of time to even things up. He turned his attention back to the card game. Or so it appeared.

CHAPTER 3

The Dining Hall was big enough to comfortably fit the roughly two hundred campers who came each week throughout the summer. This, of course, assumed that everyone sat down and stayed at their tables. A waiter system had been devised to ensure that the campers did just that. Each table in the Dining Hall had two Scouts assigned to be a waiter for each meal. The waiters were responsible for setting up, delivering the food, and clearing the table afterwards. With only the waiters walking around, it kept the aisles free from the inevitable anarchy that would result if every camper got up whenever they wanted to get something.

Each table comfortably sat about eight people. Cody and Joshua volunteered to be waiters for the first meal so that they could be seated together. The Scouts had to stay the entire week at the table which they sat at on the first day, so this ensured that Joshua and Cody would be together for the entire week. They also made sure to save a seat for Robby. Five other boys sat down at their table, and none of them, thankfully, were Levi or his entourage. Instead, Levi and his gang managed to get stuck at Pastor Bob's table, a kind of penalty for being the last ones into the Dining Hall, since his was the only table left to sit at.

CHAPTER THREE

Cody chose not to waiter his father's table. He was always cautious to maintain his distance from his father on these troop outings. As far as the troop was concerned, Cody was just one of the guys.

Cody already knew most of the other boys at his table. He had been on campouts with them before and usually hung out with them. In fact, Cody likely would have tented with a few of them if he had known that he'd be coming to camp again this summer. A bad case of the flu made that unlikely. By the time Cody got better, everyone already had a tentmate.

After the Scouts had finished piling into the Dining Hall, a camp counselor led everyone in grace. Pastor Bob dutifully and mindlessly bowed his head in reverence, as did nearly everyone in the building. But mostly people were thinking about the pizza. That was always the meal on the first day at Camp Noitanimoba. First impressions were everything, and pizza signaled a very high quality camp, as far as the Scouts were concerned. As soon as the prayer was over, everyone enthusiastically dug in.

"So, where have you been all day?" Nick Mino asked Cody, as he grabbed for a slice of pizza. A big gob of cheese goo slopped all over the shirt on his once clean Scout uniform, as he shoved the pizza slice down his mouth. Cody hurriedly finished chewing his food before answering.

"Red Feather, Robin, and I went on a hike down the Tommy Drapos Trail. Cody grabbed for his glass of juice and washed down his food before continuing. "Red Feather showed us a lot of nature stuff."

"Who?" Nick inquired with a confused look on his face.

"Oh, meet Red Feather everyone," Cody said, putting his hand on Joshua's shoulder.

"Could you pass the juice please," Robby quietly interjected.

"Good to meet you, Red Feather," Nick replied, happy to make a new friend. Nick was like that. A friend to everyone. He did have his limits, but he never showed them.

Nick then introduced the other kids at the table to Joshua. Most of them were Cody's age, around thirteen, except for Timmy Azac, who was only eleven like Robby. But Timmy had gotten in with the older Scouts right away due to his outgoing personality. He could easily pass for twelve, most of them thought.

"Why do they call you Red Feather?" Nick asked after finishing the introductions. "Are you a real Native American?" he added excitedly.

"Please pass the juice," Robby quietly repeated to no one in particular.

"Well, I'm only part. . . . ," Joshua let out before Cody jumped in.

"He knows everything about Indians and nature. He's a virtual encyclopedia. Aren't you, Red Feather?"

"Cool! Hey, Timmy is in Greenpeace," said Nick, looking over to Timmy. "Right, Timmy?"

"Could I please have some juice?" Robby muttered even more softly than before.

"Yeah, my family and I are members. I got them to join. I want to do some of that stuff when I grow up--ride ships, save whales, that kind of thing," Timmy said.

"Just a little bit of juice?" Robby peeped.

"Excuse me," Joshua interrupted. Everyone immediately gave him their attention. "Could someone please pass Robby the damn juice!"

Robby smiled.

"Oh yeah," Cody jumped in, "this is Robin."

Robby enthusiastically grabbed the juice finally coming over his way and poured it into a glass.

"Thanks," he said quietly.

"Hey!" Timmy said, "you're the kid Levi was picking on."

"Yeah," Nick added. "Don't worry about him, he picks on everyone. Just stay with us and he'll leave you alone."

They had all been harassed by Levi at one point or another. Mostly none of them ever talked about it. But things were different now. Joshua had made Levi seem less threatening. Now it seemed everyone had something to say about Levi. Each person took turns going off on him. They drew strength from each other, and for the first time none of them were afraid of Levi. Even Robby took potshots. He jumped in with his unflattering impersonation of Levi.

"Hey, you gonna cry?" Robby imitated, grunting like a Neanderthal. Everyone laughed.

They all had Joshua to thank for their new found freedom. His courage had liberated them, enabling them to discuss what had always been a humiliating topic. No one said anything to Joshua about what he had done. They didn't have to. Their admiration for him came out in the attention they gave him. Joshua felt like a celebrity. The other Scouts wanted to know everything about him. Questions just kept coming.

"Where are you from?" Nick asked.

"Why did you move?" Timmy added, before Joshua could respond to Nick's question.

"What do your parents do?" another boy jumped in.

"What are your hobbies?"

"Girlfriend?" That one came from Cody.

Joshua tensed up with the last one. He had hoped to avoid that subject. He liked his new friends and felt comfortable with them. He fit in just like one of the guys. At least he thought he did until they asked that question. It made him feel different. Joshua noted an interesting irony in the bravery everyone attributed to him. If he was so courageous and could stand up to Levi, then why couldn't he stand up for himself? Where was his courage now?

Joshua wished he could just tell everyone he was gay. But he couldn't. They were his friends, but he knew they wouldn't understand. No one would.

It wasn't difficult to change the subject, which Joshua promptly did. They talked and laughed some more, and soon dinner was over. They left the Dining Hall with everyone believing that Joshua was someone truly special, truly different. They were certainly right about that, but for different reasons.

*****

After dinner, the Scouts readied themselves for the evening campfire. Every Scout at camp made their way to the campfire "arena." The arena was basically a giant campsite fitted with log benches centered around a central "stage," which itself simply consisted of an area of cleared brush. Curtains were fastened from trees to make it look more theatrical.

The campfire program was a camp tradition. No matter how greatly summer camps varied from region to region, one could always depend on a campfire program. The format was typically the same everywhere. Camp staff took turns performing skits or singing songs. Most camps had a repertoire of skits to draw from that had been performed endlessly since time immemorial. Camp staff simply recycled the same skits over and over every couple of years. The older Scouts who had come to camp for many years could perform these skits from memory. Scoutmasters looked forward to viewing the same skits that they saw as kids performed relatively unchanged as adults.

Some of the more creative and successful camps, like Camp Noitanimoba, would alleviate the monotony of repetitive skits by offering a few of their own newly written acts. The most popular skit this year was: "Barney Goes to Jurassic Park." A counselor came on stage dressed as Barney, the lovable purple dinosaur for kids, while other staff members sang Barney's theme song. As the counselors sang the song, the campers quickly joined in. Halfway through the song a huge mock claw came from behind stage and grabbed Barney, pulling him behind the curtains. A rather loud "burp" followed shortly thereafter. The crowd roared with laughter. Sometimes the short and simple skits were the funniest. Many of the Scoutmasters laughed as well, even though most of them didn't know who Barney was.

The tone of the campfire was not all jovial. In fact, the campfire opened with the serious, almost eerie telling of the camp legend. The atmosphere invoked by the legend contrasted dramatically with the rest of the program. An older counselor walked onto stage and told a story, one that he claimed was true. Of course, the phrase, "This is a true story," commenced most horror stories, so no one was surprised when the counselor opened the camp legend in this way. It soon became apparent to the audience, however, that the counselor was not telling just another horror story. He told of something that seemed terribly real. The setting for the legend did not take place in some obscure dark mansion, or an old cemetery, as many generic ghost stories did. It took place right at Camp Noitanimoba. The staff member telling the story began to speak, and the older Scouts immediately knew that he was telling the story of Tommy Drapos. This was not fiction; it was camp history, many believed.

The narrator began by describing the young Tommy Drapos. He spoke in a loud but reverent tone. "Tommy was a young and sad 12-year-old boy. It is said that he was a quiet young lad who often stayed to himself. Other kids picked on him because of his shyness, but mostly because he was different." The counselor elaborated in vague detail. "Tommy just didn't seem to fit in," was all he said on that subject.

He continued, "While most of the boys were often playing volleyball or baseball, Tommy would just sit quietly to the side and watch. Who knows what he was thinking? Perhaps he wanted to play and have fun just like everyone else? Perhaps all he needed was for someone to take the initiative and ask him to join in? But no one cared, and Tommy continued on his own, eating alone, tenting alone, playing alone."

The audience listened intently. Joshua especially hung on to every word. There was something strangely familiar about this boy. The boy sort of reminded Joshua of Robby. Robby was different also, Joshua thought, very shy, staying to himself, at least until he and Cody had stood up for him. If only someone had been there to help Tommy. Joshua listened closely as the staff member continued the story.

"A storm descended on the camp late one evening after programming had ended. The rain had not started yet, but the lightening and thunder offered quite a show. Most people were back in their tents getting ready for bed. But Tommy was not in his tent. He was not in the campsite. Nobody knows exactly what made Tommy run off into the forest that night. Some believe his fellow Scouts had been teasing him more cruelly than usual. He ran off just to get away from them. Whatever the reason, it was the last time anyone saw Tommy alive again."

The counselor paused for a second before continuing. "For you see, Tommy Drapos became the victim of a dreadful creature that occupies these forests. No one knows what it looks like. It could be some four-legged, fanged monster that survives in the deep woods." He paused once again before continuing. "But some think its no physical creature at all." His voice began to rise, and then he poured it on. He shouted, "Some suspect this beast comes in spirit form, directly from HELL!" The counselor paused again and then lowered his voice to a whisper. "But again, no one really knows. No one has ever seen this monster and lived to tell about it."

He warned, "But what is known is that the Creature is a coward, as it attacks only helpless victims who are walking alone in the woods." The counselor stressed the word, "alone." He continued, "You could be with a big crowd, or only one other person, and you will never see the monster. But if you are alone, and it is night, you will probably be stalked, just like Tommy Drapos was stalked that night, stalked to the edge of a rock cliff and pushed over the edge of what we now call Tommy's Point."

The staff member concluded his story. "The Creature has claimed no further victims to date." He clarified: "Not because it no longer exists, but because we tell his story. We tell our Scouts never to walk off alone at night and always to travel in pairs. Most importantly, we tell our Scouts never to go to Tommy's Point. Listen to our warning and the cowardly monster will have no power over you. Do this, and there will be no further victims of the monster that haunts our Scouts."

The staff member ended the story and quietly walked off stage, leaving behind an audience of young boys determined not to be alone that night or any other. The cheerful skits which followed allowed them to temporarily forgot the fear elicited by the legend. But its lesson always lasted. The story kept kids from wandering off alone at night and getting lost or hurt. No amount of safety regulations could achieve that, and so the legend was told again every year.

At the end of the campfire program, the camp director walked on stage and went over the camp rules. Also, he briefly described the sorts of activities that the Scouts could participate in throughout the week. He then wished everyone a good night, and the Scouts were dismissed to their campsites. It was dark by then.

Pastor Bob's troop was one of the last groups out of the campfire arena, since they were seated in front. The kids slowly made their way back to camp on the long, dark path. Joshua walked with his group of friends from dinner. Most of them were reciting lines from skits that they liked. From the back, he could hear a group of kids singing the Barney song, followed by burps. Robby walked quietly next to Joshua, clinging closely to his protector.

Josh remained quiet as well. He couldn't get Tommy out of his mind. For some reason the legend got to him. He felt as though he knew Tommy. At first he thought it was because Tommy seemed so much like Robby, but now he wasn't so sure. He couldn't stop thinking about the Creature either. Joshua was not surprised that some sort of monster was in the story. After all, this was a Scout camp. Monster stories were a camp tradition. Each camp had their own version of a monster that roamed camp attacking lone Scouts who wandered off by themselves. The practical purpose of this tradition was obvious. It frightened kids and prevented them from going off on their own and getting hurt. But, in the end, these were just stories.

Still, many of these legends were based on some actual event from the camps' history. Joshua wondered if someone similar to Tommy had once existed and had fallen off of Tommy's Point. But how did he fall off? Joshua had seen Tommy's Point earlier on his hike with Cody and Robby. It didn't look that dangerous. Joshua couldn't imagine anyone accidentally falling off that cliff. Unless, Joshua reasoned, they were really being careless.

It occurred to Joshua at this point that Pastor Bob had been coming to camp for many years. Maybe, Joshua considered, he would know something about the incident.

"Pastor Bob," Joshua called.

The Pastor was right in front of Joshua, hiking steadily, beaming his flashlight ahead. He slowed as he heard his name being called from behind. He pointed his light at Josh, and recognized the new kid immediately. He prided himself in knowing everyone in his troop, by name at least.

"What is it, Joshua?" he responded.

"What really happened to Tommy?"

"Didn't you listen to the narrator?" Pastor Bob chastised. "The Creature pushed him off the cliff."

"But why?" Josh asked bewildered.

"Because he was a faggot," Pastor Bob said proudly. "Sissies don't last long in the woods," he said. "Don't worry," he continued, "I doubt you have anything to fear." Pastor Bob accepted the stereotypes about gay people. Joshua did not fit them. He had seen how Joshua courageously stood up to Levi earlier in the day. Joshua was no sissy in Pastor Bob's eyes.

Pastor Bob's response came as a shock wave to Joshua. But it made sense to him. The staff member had said that Tommy was different. Maybe that's what he meant. But why would the Creature kill gay kids?

"Oh," Joshua responded to Pastor Bob, not knowing what else to say. But Joshua now knew why Tommy had seemed so familiar. Tommy didn't remind Joshua of Robby. Tommy reminded Joshua of himself! They were both "different."

But Joshua had his friends, so he had nothing to fear according to the legend. Josh's friends not only accepted him, but they looked up to him. Joshua couldn't help but feel sorry for that lonely kid who wandered off alone into the dark. Joshua looked over to Cody and was relieved to see that his friend was so close at hand.

*****

The Scouts didn't get back to their campsite until about 10:00 p.m. A line quickly formed around the outhouse and the water pipe sticking out of the ground, which everyone jokingly referred to as "The Sink." It wasn't the most sophisticated wash area, but it was enough to clean one's hands and face and also brush one's teeth with.

Joshua, Robby, and Cody were the last in line because they waited for Robby to find his toothbrush. The Sink was only about a hundred feet from camp, but Robby didn't want to walk alone. Quite frankly, neither did Cody or Joshua.

As the three boys finished brushing, Joshua had to use the outhouse. He told Cody and Robby to go on without him and that he would only be a second. Joshua didn't mind walking alone in the dark. He spent countless times in the forest at night by himself. Night walking came easy to him. He could even walk rather effectively without a flashlight. He walked as the Native Americans did in similar situations by extending his toes first to feel the ground ahead for any impediments. If the ground was clear, then he would put the weight of his foot on his toes first and let the rest of the foot fall back. This way, one could feel any obstacles in one's way before tripping on them. It was also much quieter. Joshua had not brought his flashlight with him, and so he employed this technique as he walked back to his bunkmates. He could see the lights flashing in his tent and simply walked straight for them.

As he walked, his mind reviewed the day's events. At the beginning of the day Joshua felt completely alone and friendless. Now he had more friends than ever. He especially liked Cody. The two of them seemed to have developed a special friendship. Joshua recalled how good it felt when Cody put his hand on Joshua's shoulder earlier. He wanted Cody to do it again. Joshua imagined what it would be like to hug and even kiss Cody. But he quickly snapped out of his fantasizing as the legend of Tommy Drapos intruded upon his thoughts.

"Because he was a faggot!" Pastor Bob's words echoed in Joshua's mind.

In the distance, Joshua heard a sound. He was used to hearing all sorts of noises in the woods - from the calls of nocturnal animals to the scampering of little rodents. He had never been afraid of sounds he couldn't identify. But for some reason, there was something different about tonight. A small wave of fear reverberated through Joshua, and he quickened his pace. He stumbled a few times, but he made it back quickly.

As he reached his tent, he quickly got inside. Cody was in his boxers just getting into his sleeping bag. Robby had already fallen comfortably asleep. Joshua quickly undressed and slipped into the security of his own sleeping bag.

"Goodnight, Red Feather," Cody whispered, as he closed his eyes.

"Goodnight, Cody," Josh returned.

It had been a great day. Joshua's thoughts focused on Cody as he drifted off to sleep. He wasn't quite sure what he was feeling, because he never really felt this way before. Love, perhaps?

The legend of Tommy Drapos resounded through Josh's mind as he drifted off to sleep. He couldn't shake the story, no matter how hard he tried. The last thing in Joshua's mind before drifting off to sleep was an image of a young, frightened boy, an image he had never seen before. But somehow Josh immediately recognized the image as that of Tommy Drapos.

*****

Tommy Drapos stood helpless before his fellow Boy Scouts. They had cornered him against a tree and took turns taunting him with words like "faggot" and "queer."

"Hey, here's your best friend," one boy teased, holding up a long thick stick.

The other boys simply laughed.

"Yeah, I bet you really miss it!" another boy shouted.

Little Tommy Drapos' eyes lit up in fear as he realized what they were going to do. He cried out for mercy.

"Please stop," he whimpered between his sniffs in a barely audible voice.

CHAPTER THREE

His cries for mercy accomplished nothing.

"Hey, can't you see how sad he is?" the boy with the stick said to his crowd of friends. "I think he really misses his friend."

"Give it to him!" another boy shouted.

"Yeah, give it to him!" the crowd collectively agreed.

Two boys stepped towards Tommy's cowering body. They grabbed his arms and Tommy cried out.

"Stop it! Please, stop it!"

Some boys in the crowd repeated Tommy's words with a babyish tone, furthering Tommy's humiliation. "Top it, pwease top it," they taunted.

A third boy approached the panic stricken boy. He grabbed Tommy's pants and yanked them down. The crowd laughed. Tommy knew what they were going to do, and he was helpless to stop them.

Suddenly everything went dark. An inhuman roar emanated from the forest surrounding them. Joshua woke up with sweat pouring down his face. He wasn't sure if he had heard the sound for real or in his dream. Cody and Robby were peacefully asleep; obviously they had heard nothing.

*****

Joshua got up early the next morning. He quickly pulled on some shorts and slipped into a t-shirt and made his way to the lake. The mist was beautiful as it rolled off the water. Bird calls dominated the morning symphony, as they called and sang to each other in what sounded like hundreds of different instruments.

"Are you okay?" Cody asked Joshua, as he approached from behind.

"I thought you were still asleep," Joshua said, surprised to see Cody.

"I heard you leave the tent and got up. You tossed and turned all night. I thought something might be wrong."

Joshua didn't respond. Instead, he took advantage of his surroundings to change the subject.

"There must be hundreds of different species of plants and animals around us," Joshua said. "They are all different from each other, and yet they all work together to survive. These plants, for example, could not exist without the carbon dioxide coming from the animals," he said, as he pointed to a nearby chipmunk.

"Yeah," said Cody getting into this. "And animals need the oxygen produced by plants."

"Exactly!" said Joshua. "Everything depends on something else, something that is different from itself."

Cody put his arm on Joshua's shoulder. It was obvious to Cody that Joshua didn't want to talk about what was bothering him.

"We better get back to camp," Cody said. "It's almost time for breakfast."

As the two walked back to main camp together, Joshua allowed the legend of Tommy Drapos to slip away deep into his subconsious. Now Joshua just wanted to think about Cody.

CHAPTER 4

The first full day of regular camp programming began immediately after breakfast on Monday morning. For most of the Scouts this entailed working on merit badges. Camp offered a wide diversity of badges, something even the laziest of Scouts could get excited about. Camp was divided into several thematic areas, each offering merit badges suitable to its subject. The Ecology area, for example, offered everything from Environmental Science and Reptile Study to Astronomy and Wilderness Survival. The Aquatics area offered Swimming and Lifesaving, as well as various boating merit badges like Rowing and Canoeing. The Scoutcraft area offered Pioneering and Orienteering merit badges, while it also taught outdoor cooking skills.

The less motivated Scouts seemed to gravitate towards the Handicraft area. Badges like Basketry and Woodcarving were offered there. Many of the Handicraft badges could be earned in one or two days and thus had a reputation for being easy. Joshua had no doubt that Levi and his friends were headed toward the Handicraft area at that very moment.

Joshua, Robby, and Cody took the merit badges more seriously. The camp environment presented an excellent opportunity to earn badges that were more difficult to complete in a more urban environment, especially the nature orientated badges. Some of these badges were required if one wanted to earn the rank of Eagle Scout. The three boys thus targeted these specific required badges. The first badge they decided to take, however, had nothing to do with nature. Citizenship merit badge, started promptly at 9:00 a.m.

Traditionally, summer camps did not offer this badge, but the camp staff happened to have a college history major on it who was willing to teach it. Since Pastor Bob normally taught the badge back at home, the boys figured they could take it at camp and bypass having to take it with Pastor Bob.

A crowd had already collected by a bunch of picnic tables in front of the Dining Hall where the badge took place. As the three boys approached the tables, they saw a few kids and a counselor sitting down waiting for everyone to arrive. Joshua smiled as he saw Nick and his other mealtime friends already at the tables. Joshua tapped Nick on the shoulder as he sat down next to him. Robby and Cody perched down beside him as well. The merit badge counselor began immediately after his watch had beeped. He liked everything to happen exactly on time.

"I'm Jim Meeder," he said, "and this is Citizenship in the Nation."

Joshua figured that Jim was probably around nineteen or twenty years old.

"During the week, we will learn about what it means to be a good citizen in America." He continued, "I would like to start off by asking you what comes to your mind when you think of America?"

Several of the kids raised their hands, including Nick.

"You," Jim Meeder said, pointing to a kid from another troop.

CHAPTER FOUR

"Freedom," the boy responded mechanically, as if reading from a book.

"Very good!" Jim Meeder responded excitedly. "Freedom is the most important principle in America. That's what this country was founded on." Jim was obviously enthusiastic about his subject. Most of the kids did not really want to be at this badge. They were only taking it to meet a requirement. But as they listened to Jim, they realized that at least they weren't going to fall asleep.

"Our ancestors," continued Jim, "came over from Europe to escape persecution and to practice freedom and equality."

Joshua already began to have problems with Jim's lecture. Josh's ancestors were mostly Ojibwa.

"Eventually," Jim continued, "everyone came to believe that all people were equal and so began the American Revolution. It was a revolution to free everyone from the cruel tyranny of an oppressive government."

For a moment, Joshua thought Jim was going to stand up, put his hand over his heart, and recite the pledge of allegiance. Joshua listened intently to everything Jim said, quietly disagreeing. Joshua knew that Jim was leaving something out, something very important. The other boys had no clue that Jim's soliloquy was less than complete. They had heard the same story many times before in their school history classes. But Joshua had learned a different story. Not because he had studied more history than Jim Meeder, but because he had studied it from a different perspective. Joshua's heroes had never been people like George Washington or Thomas Jefferson. These leaders seemed distant and remote; they had little bearing on Joshua's life. Joshua had grown up inspired by a deep reverence for nature and his own culture, a culture excluded from the story that Jim was preaching.

Joshua had to say something. He never considered that his addition to the discussion might not be welcome. Joshua raised his hand furiously, and Jim called on him.

"What about the Native Americans?" Joshua asked, believing his question said everything.

Jim seemed confused by the question, as did the other kids.

"What about them?" Jim responded. "We are talking about America now," he said in a dismissive manner. Jim continued his lecture believing he had put to rest this minor annoyance. "Now, after America obtained its freedom from England," Jim said, "they began to expand westward."

Josh didn't like being dismissed, especially when he was right. Joshua could handle disagreement, but not dismissal. Normally Joshua was able to control his anger, but this issue had always been sensitive for him. Joshua raised his hand again, and this time he didn't wait to be called upon.

"The Indians were Americans!" Joshua interrupted. "They were the FIRST Americans." Joshua realized that he had everyone's attention and began a speech of his own. "They were the ones who believed in freedom. They had democracy before the United States even existed."

Josh thought Jim would stop him, but he didn't. Jim was paralyzed by cognitive dissonance. He didn't know what to do, so he did nothing. Taking advantage of Jim's frozen state, Joshua continued. "The Europeans who came over to America did not believe in freedom or equality," Josh said angrily. "They came over here and slaughtered the Indians, with the help of enslaved Africans, and women who were considered no better than property."

Josh's rejoinder stunned the other boys in class. His message didn't matter so much as the way he delivered his rebuttal. He was debating, challenging the counselor in charge. And as near as anyone could tell, Josh seemed to be winning. The Scouts quietly listened to Joshua, afraid to do anything else, secretly admiring his courage.

Jim looked furious. He regained his composure and angrily interrupted Josh's speech. "America brought civilization and Christianity to these lands!" He lowered his voice and added, "It's sad what happened to the Indians, but they are gone, and we are here today!" Jim thought that would settle matters.

"It's sad what happened to the Indians?" Joshua repeated. "Hello," he continued sarcastically, "nothing happened to me. Sitting right here."

"You know what I mean," Jim responded. "We are here today to celebrate what we became. That is what the Boy Scouts of America exemplifies," he explained.

The boys knew that Jim had won for now. He had been caught off guard by Joshua, but he was angry and had reasserted his authority. There was nothing Joshua could do but remain quiet.

But Joshua did not remain quiet. A fire raged within him. Sometimes he just couldn't control himself. "Sounds more like the Bigot Scouts of America to me," Joshua muttered to his friends, not caring if Jim heard. Jim did hear, and so did the rest of the class. Jim couldn't contain his anger anymore and expelled Joshua from the badge for the rest of the week. The other Scouts remained perfectly quiet as Joshua picked up his things and left without saying another word. But as he walked away, he felt good about what he had done. He stood up for the truth, for what was right. The boys had already seen him do that when he had defended Robby, and they were euphoric to see him in action again. He stared down bullies, and he challenged authority. Joshua was the closest thing to being a hero that any of them had ever seen.

*****

Joshua walked by himself over to the Trading Post. The Trading Post competed with the Aquatics area for most popular spot at camp. It was a little oasis in the woods. Though little more than a shack, it kept well-stocked with everything a camper needed for badges throughout the week, including tree identifications books and basketry supplies for the Handicraft area merit badges.

It also contained items which a camper might need if his own equipment failed him, such as new flashlight batteries. But these items were not what drew most people to the Trading Post. Only pop and candy could do that, and the Trading Post was well-stocked with both.

But hunger hadn't driven Joshua to the Trading Post this early in the morning; he just needed to kill some time. It was only 9:20 a.m. by the time he arrived at the Trading Post, and his friends wouldn't be done with Citizenship until 10:00 a.m. when they would be released for their next badge. The Trading Post was seldom crowded at this time of day. Most people were still full from breakfast.

Joshua took his time looking over the goods before selecting a candy bar and a can of grape soda. He sat down on the picnic table in front of the building and waited for his friends. Unfortunately, it wasn't his friends who were coming his way from the Handicraft area.

CHAPTER FOUR

Joshua considered leaving the area after he recognized the approaching Scouts. But he knew they had already seen him. He would have to confront them again. Joshua had no problem with that. He preferred to avoid a bad situation if possible, but he wasn't scared of Levi.

Levi saw Joshua sitting by himself and thanked God for the wondrous opportunity it presented. Levi always looked out for such fortuitous occurrences. This talent made Levi a superior leader for his gang. Joshua sat there alone without his friends for support. He was outnumbered three to one and had no hope of winning. These were the kind of odds Levi liked.

"Indian Boy!" Levi called to Josh. "Did you lose your friends already?"

Joshua tasted his pop, ignoring Levi.

Levi expected this, and he knew how to counter. He would have to keep at it until Joshua could no longer discount him, until acknowledgment of Levi's harassment became less painful.

"Hey, that soda looks great," Levi said, trying another tactic. "I think I'd like a soda. Have you got any change?" he asked in a threatening manner.

"Sorry," Josh responded sarcastically. "I already spent it."

"Too bad," Levi said, not giving in. "I guess I'll just have to take your soda then."

Joshua had enough. Still angry over his earlier run-in with Jim Meeder, Joshua's patience had exhausted itself. He spit in his pop, slammed it down, and stood up, angrily facing Levi. "Then try taking it!" he shouted.

"Three against one," Levi responded. "I think you have a problem."

"Don't you think I'm a little too old?" Josh said. "I mean, don't you usually pick on younger kids who can't fight back?" Josh asked sarcastically, hoping to embarrass Levi.

Levi didn't bite. "Oh yes, I was so touched when you jumped to little Robin's rescue, chivalry at its best. So, how is your little boyfriend anyway? Did you two sleep well together last night?"

Homosexual insinuations inevitably angered everyone. And the insinuation could not be ignored. It always had to be denied. But Joshua did not deny it. He simply turned and walked away. He could have stayed and continued the insult match, but it got uncomfortably personal for him. He knew what Levi was doing. Levi didn't know Josh was gay. But the subject scared Joshua. What if he said something that gave himself away? He needed to get out of there.

"Where are you going? Are you looking for your boyfriend!?" Levi shouted, as Joshua walked away.

"Go to hell!" Josh yelled back.

Levi and his friends laughed. It wasn't quite what they wanted, but at least they made Joshua mad. For now Levi had gained back some face. Only later would Levi realize that Joshua failed to deny being gay.

Joshua headed back to his campsite to wait for his friends. There was no one on the trail. Everyone was at merit badges. Josh heard people talking in the distance through the trees. As he walked alone, he reflected on his close call. He wasn't used to this obsession with homosexuality that everyone seemed to have. For the first time in his life, Josh had to deal with the bigotry that he only intellectually knew existed before.

Suddenly Joshua heard a sound. It wasn't the voices of other campers in the distance. It wasn't an animal rustling in the bushes. It was something he had heard only once before, the night before. Joshua ran anxiously back to his campsite.

*****

Robby and Cody bolted back to camp after Citizenship merit badge ended. The two were out of breath when they arrived. Joshua was quietly laying on his sleeping bag, as his two friends entered excitedly. Robby, exhausted, collapsed on his sleeping bag. Cody, however, survived the run in a little better shape, and stuck to the plan at hand. He lavished Joshua with attention.

"That was great!" Cody said to Josh. "Everyone was talking about you after the badge ended."

"Yeah, the rebel strikes again," Joshua responded humorously. "How did the rest of class go?" he added, quickly changing the subject.

"Pretty boring without you there," Robby managed to wheeze between gasps.

Cody filled Joshua in. "Jim lectured about patriotism after you left. He said that many people, like you, needed to learn history."

Robby and Cody didn't accept anything Jim had said. Jim knew a lot of things as a teacher, but as their friend, Joshua had better qualifications.

"We're not going back tomorrow," Cody said. Robby nodded in agreement. "If you're a subversive, then so are we," Cody teased.

"Yeah," Robby agreed.

Joshua burst out laughing. Cody and Robby looked at each other with surprise.

"What's so funny?" asked Cody.

Joshua could barely respond, as he rolled on his sleeping bag with laughter. "I just got this image of Robby in his Robin costume preaching communist propaganda."

They all joined in on the laughter, sharing the ridiculous image. Robby laughed the hardest, although he really had no idea what a communist or a subversive was.

The laughter didn't last long.

"Where the hell is Cody!" the three tentmates heard Pastor Bob shout to some of the boys outside the tent.

"In his tent," one boy immediately responded, effortlessly betraying his troopmates, as he pointed to Cody's tent. He knew he just got brownie points for that one.

"Shit," Joshua whispered frantically. "Do you think he heard already?"

Then they made out Levi's voice talking with his gang in the background. There was no question as to who had given them away. News traveled fast at camp, and once Levi got wind of what happened to Joshua witht the Citizenship instructor, he went straight to Pastor Bob with it.

"Don't worry," Cody said, trying to calm his friends. "He's my father, I know how to handle him. Let me do the talking. Okay?"

"No argument from me," Joshua said.

They didn't wait for Robby to respond.

The tent door flew open, and a furious Pastor Bob shot his head inside.

"Damn it, Joshua!" he shouted. "I heard you were causing trouble at Citizenship merit badge!"

Cody knew this had to be handled delicately. Citizenship was his father's specialty. Patriotism was as much a religion to his father as was Christianity. He wasn't about to respond kindly to any talk about oppressing Indians.

"Dad, hi, come in," Cody said innocently.

Joshua and Robby sat there with nervous expressions on their faces, but they did not say a word.

"We were just talking about you," Cody continued. "I was telling Joshua and Robby about all the cool war stories that you tell when teaching Citizenship merit badge back at home."

Cody knew this would get his father's attention. Though his service was only peacetime, Pastor Bob always liked to talk about his involvement in the armed forces as though he had seen hard combat. He never actually lied, but he was prone to exaggeration and misdirection.

Pastor Bob was completely disarmed.

"We all decided that we'd rather take Citizenship merit badge from a real hero," Cody continued, "not some boring college student."

Robby nodded his head excitedly in agreement.

Pastor Bob didn't know what to say. Instinctively he replied, "Yeah, well, you know college students get everything from a textbook, no real life experience. That's the problem with them."

Robby again nodded his head in agreement, and this time Joshua joined him.

"So what did you want to talk with Joshua about, Dad?"

"Oh, nothing," Pastor Bob responded embarrassingly. "Just like to keep track of everyone, that's all."

"See you all later," he said, as he retreated from the tent.

The tension level crashed as Cody's father left the room.

"Skillful to the max," Joshua said.

Robby nodded in agreement. Cody had easily manipulated and disarmed his father. For the moment, Cody was the hero.

*****

The rest of the morning passed without incident. The boys had gone to Environmental Science merit badge at 10:00 a.m. and Indian Lore at 11:00 a.m. Unlike Citizenship, Joshua was very excited about both of those badges. He actually learned a lot of things he hadn't known before. The counselor for this badge was a welcome relief from Jim Meeder. He had a genuine respect for Native American customs. Joshua started to realize that these badges might actually be fun.

At lunch time, Joshua and his new friends all sat together again. The incident with Jim Meeder only occupied a brief moment of their conversation. Oddly enough, Robby became the center of attention at the meal. By now, Robby had added Pastor Bob and Jim Meeder to his repertoire of impressions. He mimicked them perfectly.

"Where the hell is Joshua?!" Robby shouted, sounding eerily like Pastor Bob." All the boys laughed. Robby seemed to have completely left his shell, and the boys responded positively. They liked anyone who could make them laugh as hard as Robby did.

As they left the Dining Hall after lunch, Timmy and Nick invited Robby to join them at Canoeing merit badge. Robby immediately accepted the invitation before realizing he had already agreed to hike with Joshua and Cody again. They noticed his predicament and motioned for him to go. They were glad to see Robby making friends.

CHAPTER FOUR

The group agreed to meet later for the "free swim" period at 3:00 p.m. That gave Josh and Cody two hours for their hike. The group split off into two groups, and Josh and Cody walked off by themselves into the woods.

The nature hike was a good excuse to meet some of the requirements for Environmental Science merit badge. They had to put in a total of eight hours of observation in nature during the course of the week and write a report based on their findings. The requirements called for them to observe which environmental factors determined the kinds of wildlife they saw during their observations. Most of the Scouts simply made stuff up.

After about fifteen minutes of hiking away from main camp, Joshua and Cody noticed there were no campsites or campers around anymore. It was the first time they had been truly alone together since they met.

Cody seemed preoccupied. He had been fine up until they left main camp together. Then he got real quiet. Joshua continued to point out interesting items in nature as he came across them, even though he knew Cody wasn't really paying attention.

"This is one of my favorites," Joshua said, as he picked a glove-shaped leaf. Joshua broke the stem from the leaf in half and put it up to Cody's nose. "Smell this," he offered.

Cody took a curious whiff. He was obviously pleased with the sweet perfume like fragrance.

"Sassafras," Joshua said.

Cody seemed to lose interest again, but Joshua tried to hold his attention.

"Pioneers used to make root beer from it," Josh continued. Cody feigned attention.

Josh couldn't ignore Cody's silence any longer. He started to get worried. At first he thought Cody was just being shy, but something really seemed to be bothering him.

"Are you okay, Cody?" Joshua finally asked.

Joshua's question surprised Cody. He didn't realize he had been wearing his preoccupation like a badge. Instinctively, Cody almost dismissed Josh's concern with the cliché response: "Yeah, I'm fine." But Cody had come to trust Joshua, even though he had only known him for short time

"Do you believe in the camp monster?" Cody asked, hoping Joshua could reassure him that the monster didn't exist.

At first the question surprised Joshua, but then he realized it made sense. The two were alone together in the woods away from main camp. It was only natural that Cody would be thinking about the legend. Joshua had almost entirely forgotten about it and his dream the night before. It seemed like it happened ages ago.

"Don't worry, we're not alone," Joshua said, hoping to reassure Cody. "The legend says that the Beast only attacks those who are alone."

"But do you believe in him?" Cody asked again.

"Indians believe in a type of spirit, the Maji-Manitoo, or bad spirit," Josh informed Cody. "But I don't know. I mean, all legends have a bit of truth," Joshua said. "I'm sure that Tommy Drapos probably fell off the cliff, but I'm not so sure that. . ."

Joshua paused. He realized that he was about to bring up a taboo subject, one that could give him away. But for some reason, he continued. He had grown to trust Cody, and despite his better instincts, Joshua finished his sentence. "I'm not sure that what your father said was true."

CHAPTER FOUR

Cody knew what he meant. He had been there last night when his father said that the Creature killed Tommy Drapos because he was gay. But Cody feigned ignorance, hoping not to appear as though he brought up the subject.

"What do you mean?" Cody replied innocently.

"Well, maybe Tommy Drapos was. . ." Josh paused again, but he was determined to finish this increasingly awkward conversation. It was now or never. "...gay," he said, finishing his sentence and half expecting the world to end. It didn't. Cody kept listening intently to Josh's every word. He did a good job of acting like he wasn't uncomfortable.

"But even if he was gay, I don't think it was right for the kids to pick on him. And I certainly don't think that there is any creature out there attacking gay kids; it doesn't make sense."

Cody jumped in, anxious to add his thoughts. "My father says that God sent the Creature after gays, because gays don't follow God's laws," he replied. But Cody was relieved to hear Joshua defend Tommy. It was the first time he had ever heard anyone defend a gay person in his entire life. People just didn't think like that in his house.

"Indians didn't hate gay people," Josh offered shyly. "They believed they were given a special power by the Creator. They were highly revered."

"Of course, I don't believe. . ." Cody said timidly and then stopped. It was his turn to pause. His body tensed up, and he began to shake. "I don't believe everything my father says." He breathed in deeply and let it out. He had fully intended to stop there and say no more. But he continued. He added something that he never thought he'd say in his entire life. Something which Joshua made it seem natural for him to say.

65

"I think I'm gay," Cody said, as he gazed in Josh's eyes.

Joshua stopped and faced Cody. He could not believe Cody just told him that. Not only hadn't he even suspected that Cody was gay, but he didn't think it was possible for anyone to have the courage to say it. He saw Cody standing there shaking, desperately wondering how Joshua would respond. Josh had to say something.

"And you guys thought I was a hero," Joshua finally said. "I don't think I could have said that first," he added, hoping Cody would get the point.

"You mean," Cody began to inquire with genuine shock. "You are too?"

"Yeah," Joshua confirmed. "I guess we really do have a lot in common."

They had both conquered their worst fears without ever really intending to. They told each other their deepest secret. They could trust each other no matter how bad things got.

They quickly became more comfortable with the subject. Once the fear of being found out was gone, they found it easy to discuss. They had a million questions for each other.

"When did you first know?" one asked.

"Does anyone else know?" the other inquired.

The most important question was the one that started the whole conversation, the one about Tommy Drapos. "Do you believe in the Creature?" No matter how strange, no matter how much it didn't make sense, Cody had to answer, "Yes." Tommy was killed for being gay, and God allowed this to happen. Cody didn't know much about the Bible, but he had heard preachers and his own father go off on homosexuals enough to know what happened to them when they died.

CHAPTER FOUR

Another thought had also gone through Cody's mind. His father once said that God punishes gays since they chose to sin against God. Cody didn't understand that. His father actually thought that gay people chose to be gay. God didn't want anyone to make such a choice. That's why they were going to Hell, according to Cody's father.

Cody knew for a fact that he did not choose to be attracted to other boys. He couldn't even conceive of such a thing. He wondered if his father could choose to be attracted to guys. Of course, his father would deny such a possibility for himself, but not for gay people.

Cody knew his father was wrong about it being a choice. And if his father was wrong about this, Cody thought, maybe he was also wrong about God hating gays and maybe even about the Creature.

Cody began to explain these thoughts to Joshua and was relieved that Joshua seemed to agree. He was especially interested in hearing that the Native Americans didn't believe God hated gays.

In fact, gay people were venerated and often made holy men, or shaman, in Native American societies. They were called "Niizh manidoowag" or Two-Spirits," Joshua informed Cody. Such people, it seemed, were considered to have a very close and special relationship with God. This revelation was comforting to Cody.

Time stood still for the two as they hiked and discussed this previously taboo subject with each other. The alarm on Cody's watch beeped, reminding them of the time.

"It's 3:00 p.m. already!" Joshua said excitedly.

"We're late for swimming!" Cody realized, as he remembered they were supposed to meet their friends at the lake.

"Thanks," Cody said to Joshua, as he put his hand on Joshua's shoulder.

"No problem, bro," Josh responded, gladly putting his arm around Cody as they started back to camp. It was the first time they felt good about what they were, and the first time either of them had truly acknowledged their sexual orientation to someone else. It was an unbelievably good first day at camp.

CHAPTER 5

Joshua and Cody were about twenty minutes late by the time they arrived at the lakefront for the free swim period. Robby and his new friends were already swimming when the two arrived. Cody and Joshua noticed that they were playing water tag, and Robby appeared to be "it." Robby would swim with all his might to the last location where he saw someone, only to discover them gone by the time he arrived. But Robby never seemed to get frustrated at his inability to catch anyone. He thrived on the attention he got from being "it."

Timmy slowly crept up behind Robby and started splashing him. By the time Robby turned around, Timmy had ducked under water and made his escape. Robby went after him. He knew that Timmy would probably be his best chance at catching someone, since they were the same age. He was right. He lunged forward and tagged Timmy on the foot as Timmy tried to get away. Robby then swam frantically to shore so as to avoid a counter-tag. He quickly got out of the lake and noticed Joshua and Cody arriving.

Cody and Josh entered the swimming area, and Robby ran up to them. He was out of breath.

"Where you guys been?" he asked between pants.

Cody looked at Joshua and smiled.

"We kinda lost track of time," Josh explained.

"Well, get in!" Robby yelled, as he ran back into the water. The rest of the gang waved for them to join. Cody and Joshua pulled off their shirts and jumped in.

The designated swimming area was crowded this afternoon, containing nearly fifty kids. Each Scout troop at camp had been assigned one of two swim periods so as to split the numbers up. The swimming area would have been too crowded if all the troops came in at the same time.

The cold water surprised Joshua at first, but he quickly got used to the temperature. Somehow Joshua became "it" by virtue of his being late. He carefully scanned the area for potential targets. Unfortunately, he noticed Levi and his band approaching the beach. Josh and his friends ceased playing, one by one, as they saw Levi enter the area. Robby spoke first.

"Something really reeks!" Robby said out loud. Joshua noted how bold Robby had become. Just the day before little Robby had been afraid to talk.

Fortunately, the swimming area was pretty big, and Levi and his friends entered at the other end. As long as he and his gang stayed to themselves, no conflict need arise. Just the same, Joshua kept an eye out for Robby as they continued to play tag. It wasn't long before the boys became totally engrossed in their game once again.

Levi and his buddies began playing water basketball at the other end of the swimming area. A basketball hoop hung from the dock. Levi's followers seemed equally engrossed in their game, which helped Joshua and his friends relax a bit. Of course, this is just what Levi wanted, to catch his unsuspecting targets off-guard. Levi slowly positioned himself closer to Josh's side of the swimming area. Suddenly he took a deep breath and went underwater.

Robby was "it" again. Tommy had tagged his leg under water after Robby splashed him from behind. Robby didn't even notice how tired he had become. He was having too much fun. A huge smile beamed across his face as he surfaced realizing he was "it" again. He seemed to like that position the best. He looked around for potential targets. Cody was the furthest away from him, and Tommy had quickly made his get-away. Nick was taunting him with splashes about ten feet away but was too close to the beach. Nick could easily get out of the water and run further away.

Robby finally decided to target Joshua. He was also about ten feet away but in deeper water. Robby prepared to dive after Josh when Levi suddenly lunged out of the water from behind him. Levi's left arm wrapped around Robby's throat, and his right arm pushed down on Robby's head. The two boys both went under. Robby was so shocked that he had no time to take a breath. He panicked and struggled furiously to get a gulp of air. But it was of no use. Levi was too strong, and he held Robby down with a steel grip and a smirk of satisfaction. Robby gulped down water, much of it rushing into his lungs.

Robby didn't remember surfacing. All he knew was that he couldn't breath, as he coughed furiously, while Levi stood behind him laughing. Joshua quickly swam over to Robby and tried to take him to shore. The other boys quickly swam over to help. A lifeguard ran from the dock and onto the beach as he observed what had happened. He witnessed the entire incident.

Joshua had never felt so much anger in his life. After seeing that Robby was going to be all right, he shot Levi a fierce glance.

"Get the hell out of here, now!" Josh heard a voice scream. He noticed the lifeguard shouting frantically at Levi. Joshua wanted to handle the situation himself, but he wasn't about to argue with a counselor again after the incident with the Citizenship merit badge instructor.

"What?" Levi said innocently. He quickly pleaded, "He's from my troop; we are friends. It was just a joke." His pleading sounded astonishingly sincere.

But it didn't work. The lifeguard reached Levi, grabbed him by the shoulder, and proceeded to drag him to shore.

Another lifeguard shouted at Levi's friends. "All of you, get out!"

It was their turn to feign ignorance. "But we didn't do anything," they argued.

"Get out!" The lifeguard screamed again, not listening to their pleas.

The gang reluctantly got out of the lake, put on their shirts, and made their way to the exit, where Levi was being reprimanded by the first lifeguard. The lifeguard told them all not to bother coming back during the week. Levi was the only one that had a smile on his face as they left. He had gotten Robby real good and expected his friends to be pleased. He was surprised when they turned on him.

"Thanks a whole fucking lot!" one of them yelled. None of them were accustomed to telling off Levi. They never even considered it before, as they assumed no one would back them up. But Joshua's earlier confrontation with Levi made him seem a little more human. Add that to the fact that they had all just been expelled from the beach all week and one had a recipe for a coup. Most of Levi's gang had signed up for Aquatics area merit badges, and they would not be allowed to take them now.

"What?" Levi said to his angry friends, again pleading innocent. "I was just settling an old score," he added, expecting that to be enough. He then tried to change the subject. "Come on, let's find something else to do." He began to walk and was surprised to discover that no one followed. All his friends had angry looks on their faces. Apparently, they expected a better explanation.

Joshua and friends quickly left the beach after the incident. Robby was no longer in the mood for swimming after all his hacking, and the rest of the boys were not about to continue swimming without their friend.

Levi took this opportunity to regain face with his group. He knew his friends could not resist joining with him in a little game of humiliation.

Robby coughed a little as he walked with his friends away from the beach. Cody had his hand on Robby's back, occasionally patting it.

"Can't you swim?" Levi yelled over to them. Levi laughed and with a nod invited his friends to join in. They simply ignored Levi. Joshua didn't. He was enraged. His eyes engaged Levi's, as he walked toward him. He was so angry he didn't even notice that Robby was ahead of him.

"You fucking asshole!" Robby shouted at the top of his lungs. This outburst surprised Levi more than anyone. He had expected to get yelled at by Joshua but not some frail wimp like Robby. The whole world seemed to be going mad.

Joshua's anger transformed instantly into shock and then concern for Robby. Joshua ran to catch up with him before he got himself killed.

Robby began to cough frantically. But he didn't look helpless. He looked angry. And in that anger and in between coughs he did the unthinkable and managed to cry out, "You stupid bastard!" Robby seemed to have mastered an expressive vocabulary from his newest friends.

Levi quickly recovered his senses and knew he had to do something. His friends were abandoning him. And a little punk needed to be put in his place.

"Get the hell out of here!" Joshua threatened.

Levi again glanced over to his friends for support. They just stood there staring at him, waiting to see what he would do next. Levi didn't know what to do. This was not part of the game. He had no experience being the outsider. His pool of games and tricks offered him no clue as to how to respond. He was alone. Levi turned and walked away quickly. A tear began to well up in his eye, but no one noticed.

*****

Everyone discussed Robby's confrontation with Levi at dinner. They couldn't believe the power shifts that had occurred at camp so far this week. First, Joshua did the unthinkable by standing up to Levi. Now, small wimpy kids like Robby were directly confronting him. Anyone who valued their money would avoid trying to predict normal events this week.

Robby felt proud of himself for the first time in his life. He hadn't intended to confront Levi. Anger drove him. But Robby had been angry before and never acted this way. His friends, especially Joshua, triggered a latent courage within him. They gave him a boost of self-esteem that had always been lacking. He stood up for himself because he now realized he was worth standing up for. Robby knew that Joshua was responsible for that, and Robby didn't intend on forgetting that anytime soon. Neither did the other boys at the table.

"Hey, Robin," Timmy called, "I think you are taking this vigilante stuff too seriously. Let Batman do some of the work," he teased.

"Or try using your Bat Utility Belt," Nick added. "Do some major damage."

Everyone laughed. Robby just smiled. He was enchanted by all the attention, and his face turned red.

"Could you pass the juice please," he asked, hoping someone would change the subject.

"Here you go," said Nick, immediately passing the drink to Robby.

"Allow me," Tommy said grabbing the juice. "Robin deserves to be served," he argued, as he poured the juice for Robby.

Everybody enjoyed this act. Robby's new friends treated him like a king. He felt important for the first time in his life. He enjoyed his moment in the spotlight. His friends knew this and were going to make sure he remembered it.

"Okay, enough," Cody said. "Robby's face is red enough. If it turns any redder, he won't have enough blood for the rest of his body."

Robby blushed even more.

Levi didn't seem to be having a very good time at his table. He sat with his gang and didn't say a word. His friends talked a lot, but not to Levi. The only one who spoke to Levi during the meal was Pastor Bob, who punished Levi for the swimming incident by assigning him waiter duty for the rest of the week. Pastor Bob hated it when adult leaders noticed the infractions of his kids. It made him look bad. So, Pastor Bob reacted sourly when the Camp Director himself informed him that Levi had been causing trouble at the lake. This made Pastor Bob look bad, and that he didn't like.

Levi just sat there quietly listening to his friends while they talked and laughed without his input or leadership. Over the noise of his friends, he heard the kids talking at Joshua's table. He couldn't hear exactly what they were saying, but he knew they were talking about him and about what Robby had done earlier. Each time they laughed, Levi felt even more humiliated. They were taunting him, and he was powerless to stop them. He was alone.

*****

Joshua sat at the picnic tables in front of the Dining Hall with his new friends after dinner ended. Robby was the designated waiter for their table today, and the group waited for him to finish up. They didn't realize that Levi had been made permanent waiter for his table, and that Robby would be in the Dining Hall alone with Levi. Even if they did know, they would not have been worried about Robby. After his last encounter with Levi, he clearly demonstrated that he could take care of himself.

Without Robby to perform his imitations of Levi, or Pastor Bob, the conversation took on an uncharacteristically serious tone. The conversation started with Timmy asking Cody and Joshua about their afternoon hike together.

"Why were you two so late for swimming earlier today?" Timmy asked.

"Josh found a great spot for observing wildlife," Cody quickly responded. "We took some great notes for our report for Environmental Science."

CHAPTER FIVE

Cody wasn't exactly lying. The two had made plenty of observations for their report as they walked together earlier, although Joshua could have easily made all the notes up from his own previous experiences in nature.

"I remember having to do that report," Nick said. Nick was the oldest in the group and had completed the merit badge several years ago.

"You really don't have to take the report too seriously," he offered. "The counselor is pretty easy. If you hand a report in, that's basically good enough."

"We learned a lot," Cody said, although he was not talking about the badge.

Just then, Levi walked out of the Dining Hall. His friends hadn't waited for him. He looked at Josh and his group and walked the other way towards the lake. Joshua watched him carefully. As mad as Joshua was at Levi, he felt kind of sorry for him. Levi was completely alone now, kind of like Robby had been. Maybe Levi had learned his lesson, Joshua thought.

"I'll be right back," Joshua said to his friends, as he ran off towards the lake.

His friends paid little attention and continued their conversation.

*****

The lake returned naturally to its calm and peaceful state after all the kids had left it for dinner. Joshua could hardly believe it was the same lake. The tranquillity hypnotized him, and for a moment he had almost forgotten why he had come here.

Levi hadn't gone far. He found a big granite rock to sit on by the beach just outside of the swimming area. He sat there staring at the ripples in the lake. He contemplated the events that had torn him from all his friends in just a matter of hours. Now he was alone. He had no friends to lead or to goof around with. Worst of all, a eleven-year-old kid had bested him in front of everyone. Levi just stared at the water.

Levi realized that he was not alone as he saw a reflection of Joshua's face in the water. This was disconcerting, as he hadn't heard Joshua walk up behind him.

Joshua didn't know exactly what he was going to say, he wasn't even exactly sure why he was here. But something made him come. Levi was alone now, and Joshua figured maybe with all his defenses down, Levi might at least talk. About what, Joshua didn't know.

"Levi," Joshua finally called softly, as he walked up behind him.

Levi said nothing. He just kept staring at the lake as though he hadn't heard Josh.

"I saw you come down here," Joshua said. "You looked like you might want to talk."

"Leave me alone," Levi said quietly, not even turning around to acknowledge Joshua's presence.

Joshua persisted. He knew that Levi would be difficult at first. That was part of who he was. But Joshua believed there had to be something beyond that, and he was determined to reach it.

"Look, I know we got off to a bad start," Josh said, hoping to break the ice, "but maybe we could start over."

"I said leave me alone!" Levi yelled angrily, this time turning his head to face Joshua. "I'm not looking for a boyfriend!" That should have been enough, but Joshua persisted.

CHAPTER FIVE

"Hey, you can drop the act," Joshua shot back firmly. "I didn't come hear to fight, or rub it in. I just thought maybe I could help."

"You get me in trouble with Pastor Bob! You get me evicted from the lakefront! Now you want to help!" Levi turned his face away from Joshua and stared at the lake once again. "Jump off Tommy's Point," he said. "That would help."

"Levi," Joshua tried again.

"Just leave me alone!" Levi shouted angrily.

Joshua almost left after that but something made him try once again.

"My friends and I are going on the astronomy hike soon. You are. . . " Josh paused for a second. He could hardly believe what he was about to ask. Even as he finished his sentence, he wondered what had come over him. "You are welcome to come with us," he finished.

Levi could hardly believe what he heard.

"Why the fuck do you want me to come with you?"

"Well, my friends and I could always use more friends," Joshua said, extending his hand for Levi to shake.

"Friends," Joshua offered.

Joshua didn't know how Levi was going to react. At worst he figured Levi would just ignore him and keep staring at the lake. But Levi didn't ignore him.

Levi stood up and faced Joshua. He looked as mad as when he had been pushed into the fence by him during their first confrontation.

"Listen, I don't know what the fuck kind of game you think you are playing, but I'm not interested in you or your faggot friends!"

Josh could not believe this guy. Here Joshua was making a friendly gesture, and Levi reacted with anger.

"Just get out of here, and go back to your boyfriend!" he yelled.

That was it, Josh decided. Levi was now definitely on his own as far as he was concerned. He tried his best to make peace; Levi simply wasn't interested. If he wanted to be alone, fine, let him, Josh decided as he walked away.

Levi watched Joshua retreat, surprised that he left that easily. Levi had accused him of being gay. Typically that was the surest way to make someone mad. Anger was something Levi knew how to deal with. But Joshua didn't get mad, and he didn't deny being gay. It dawned on Levi that this was the second time Joshua had just walked away after Levi had made the accusation.

*****

Levi's gang headed towards the Field Sports area, which usually opened about a half-hour after dinner. Most people came to this area to practice with rifles and shotguns. The Field Sport's staff also taught archery skills, but this was less popular.

Ken Fenton had filled the power vacuum left by Levi's absence. He was a poor substitute. He could come up with ideas of things to do, but he didn't really make them fun. Levi, at least, entertained them. No matter how boring things got, Levi had always been able to make any situation fun, despite the fact that the fun was usually had at someone else's expense.

Ken couldn't take advantage of those types of situations even when they were handed to him. The gang had run across several groups of younger boys from other troops on the way to the rifle range, but the kids passed by without Ken showing the slightest interest in harassing them. One boy they ran across was completely alone. Ken said nothing as they walked by him. Levi never would have let such great luck pass him by without at least shouting out a few insults to the lone Scout. The gang began to realize how much they missed their former leader.

The Field Sports area hadn't opened yet when they arrived. They had a few minutes to wait before a staff member would come to open things up. The gang just waited there along with about ten other kids from other troops.

"Hey, let's have a towel fight," Ken desperately offered, hoping the gang would join in.

"Lame," one of the gang responded.

"We don't have our towels," another boy reminded Ken, as though Ken were a complete idiot. Some of the gang got a smirk out of this. It was obvious to a few of them that Ken wouldn't last much longer. Already, others were vying for dominance.

A kid from another troop had overheard the conversation and smirked as well. Ken could not help but notice. It was one thing for his own group to laugh at him, but it was quite another thing for a complete stranger to do so.

"What are you laughing at?" Ken challenged, as he confronted the boy. Ken thought for a second and then added: "Fag!" That was perfect, Ken thought. He had challenged another boy and accused him of being a homosexual. He had followed Levi's formula perfectly, or so he thought. Surely his gang would be impressed.

"Lay off him, Ken," one of his gang said.

"Yeah," another jumped in. "The last thing we need is to get thrown out of another area." The other boys agreed.

Ken didn't know what else to do. Nothing seemed to work, not even Levi's trusted formula. Ken just couldn't fill Levi's shoes.

Ken then noticed Levi approaching them from the path. Ken's face lit up with delight. The other kids didn't admit it, but they were glad as well.

"Hey guys," Levi said innocently, as he arrived. "I thought I might find you all here."

"Well, you certainly wouldn't find us at the beach," one of the kids chided sarcastically.

"Yup, that option no longer exists," another agreed.

"Yeah, well, I kinda wanted to apologize for getting you all in trouble," he said in a genuinely sorry tone. "It's just that it was the perfect opportunity. The little fag had his back facing me. He practically begged to get dunked."

The boys started to laugh. Evidently they agreed with Levi's assessment.

Levi continued as he realized they were buying it. "If I thought you guys would get punished, I never would have done it. The lifeguard had no right to throw you guys out."

Again the gang agreed. Levi played them perfectly. He knew that as mad as his gang was at him, they were probably equally mad at the lifeguard for blaming them. Levi's friends got mad enough when they were blamed for things they actually did, let alone getting punished for something they never thought of doing. Levi pushed all the right buttons.

"Yeah, well, the little fag did have it coming," Ken agreed, trying to help Levi's case.

"Next time wait until there is no lifeguard around," another boy added. They were obviously ready to take Levi back. A few more well-meaning taunts and the gang would be whole again.

"So, what the fuck are you looking at?" Levi yelled over to one of the boys who was waiting patiently by himself for the Field Sports area to open up.

The boys in his gang laughed. Ken stood there in awe. How the hell did Levi do it? Ken wondered to himself.

CHAPTER 6

Night finally arrived, and Josh and friends looked forward to the astronomy hike planned for later that night. Like Levi's gang, Joshua and his friends needed to kill some time. But unlike his gang, Josh's friends had fun simply hanging out together. In the process, they happened upon yet another one of Robby's quirky talents. The group had already recognized his flair for impersonations. But this latest discovery was nearly beyond belief.

"Try it again," Nick insisted, unable to accept what he had just seen.

"Yeah, let's test him again," Timmy demanded.

Robby just rolled his eyes. It was no big deal to him. But he enjoyed the attention.

Cody was the first to notice Robby's unique talent. He had been in his tent with Joshua discussing merit badge requirements, while Robby sat quietly on his sleeping bag reading his comic books. Outside the tent someone was playing a boom box that they had brought to camp. The only songs that played were from an oldies radio station in a nearby small town. Cody started to get annoyed because Robby was singing all the background songs he heard on the radio to himself, seemingly unaware of how loud he had gotten. It finally occurred to Cody that no matter how obscure the song was, Robby still knew all the words. Cody quickly brought Robby outside to test his ability with the rest of the troop. One after another the Scouts shouted out song titles from popular rock groups and listened in amazement as Robby recited from memory all the words to the song. Most of these songs were current ones that the kids all recognized.

"Do 'Rat in a Cage!'" shouted one of the Scouts.

The title was incorrect, but Robby knew which song the Scout meant. Robby immediately took his stance, gripped his hand as if holding a microphone, and began mimicking the popular song by the Smashing Pumpkins. Not only did he know the words, but he was quite an entertaining performer as well. His energetic expressions captured perfectly the spirit of each song.

As he recited the words, Robby sang in a loud scratchy voice. The other Scouts listened intently and even tried to imitate the song with him. But even the most devoted Smashing Pumpkin's fan at camp didn't know all the words. And as he continued beyond the more commonly known words, Robby realized that no one else was following along anymore.

One of the Scouts interrupted Robby halfway through the song and shouted out another song title. Soon, another Scout added one to the list. After awhile, the kids were testing the limits of Robby's ability more than they were trying to hear their favorite song.

They started with well-known groups and songs like Pearl Jam's, "Jeremy," or Nirvana's, "Smells Like Teen Spirit." Some tried a little spin on the test by shouting out cartoon theme songs like "Spider Man" or "Wonder Dog." Robby knew those too, but he especially got into "Scooby Doo."

One of the older Scouts, who was the assistant Scoutmaster, thought he could catch Robby by throwing out some obscure songs from the seventies. Cody already knew that Robby could do those as well since he had already done so in the tent.

"'Seasons in the Sun,' by Terry Jacks!" the assistant Scoutmaster shouted. He was stunned as he listened to Robby recite the exact words to this song that he himself could barely remember from his childhood.

"Good God, Robin, you must listen to a lot of music!" one Scout shouted.

"Not really," Robby said. "My brother does play MTV a lot downstairs though, while I'm studying in my room."

This amazed the Scouts the most. Robby hadn't memorized the words to any of the songs. He just heard them, sometimes only once, and knew them forever.

"'Afternoon Delight,'" the assistant Scoutmaster shouted one last time, thinking Robby couldn't possibly keep this up.

Robby thought for a second and then began. He only made it past the first line, when he was stopped.

"Ok already," the assistant Scoutmaster interrupted. "You win." He was absolutely stunned as he sat there and listened to a young kid recite the words to a song that had been a hit before Robby had even been born. Robby was indeed the best and the brightest of the MTV generation.

*****

Robby's little talent show held everyone's attention until it was time to leave for the astronomy hike. By now, Josh's new friends all knew each other pretty well. They recognized each other's interests and temperaments. They knew what was funny, and what was going too far.

Robby, for example, in addition to being a perfect mimic and having a near photographic memory, was interested in science-fiction. He could go on for hours in minute detail about any science fiction movie or television series ever made, but his specialty was Batman. His personality was rather odd at times. He seemed to love attention, but he hated being in the spotlight. Despite such contradictions, Robby seemed pretty well-adjusted.

Nick was probably the least brightest of the group, but he was the most jovial. No matter how bad a situation got, he could lighten things up. He could express an interest in whatever people were talking about at the moment, but he didn't really seem to have any interests of his own.

Timmy was often the clown of the group. He could always be counted on for a good comeback. He gladly shared his talent at making people laugh with their newest addition, Robby. Timmy's self-esteem was very high, and nothing really threatened him. He was outgoing and fun.

Everyone felt they knew Cody the best. He was everyone's friend when they needed one, even to people outside the group. Everyone felt like they could talk to Cody and trust that he would listen and understand. If things ever got bad, they knew he would be there for any of them.

Joshua was the bravest and certainly the most knowledgeable of the group. He had an answer for absolutely everything and an anecdote for every situation. He lacked the arrogance that usually accompanied such knowledge, and that made him a natural teacher. And, of course, his courage had already taken on mythic proportions.

Josh's friends were surprised to discover that it was almost 9:00 p.m. They had managed to kill over two hours without even trying. They headed towards the Dining Hall where those interested in the astronomy hike were to congregate.

A small group had already accumulated by the time they arrived. They were glad to see that Levi was not there. The kids wanted to enjoy this hike.

Robby and Joshua probably anticipated the hike the most, but for different reasons. Robby's passion for science fiction had prompted him to study astronomy whenever he had the chance. He knew all about nebulas and galaxies and could even discuss black holes and cosmic strings. Unfortunately, the group would not be seeing any of those things tonight, but this didn't silence Robby's active imagination.

Joshua was attracted more to the aesthetic qualities of the night sky. His astronomical knowledge was less abstract and scientific than Robby's. He focused more on the visible night sky. He could identify many stars, planets, and constellations by sight. He also knew many of the myths associated with them.

The Astronomy merit badge counselor arrived, and the group immediately set off on their journey. Stars were just emerging, as the sun descended further into night, and the group began their hike.

Main camp was well lit by lights, masking what little of the night sky they could see through the trees. It was even worse when they got to "the Desert," where the parking lot lights gave everyone day vision. But as they continued down the path away from main camp, the darkness grew like a living thing. Soon, they were completely engulfed by it.

CHAPTER SIX

The counselor wouldn't let anyone use flashlights. This would only prevent their eyes from adjusting to the dark. They were heading out to a nearby open field, and he wanted the Scouts to have night vision by the time they arrived.

Once they got on the trail to the field, their eyes finally began to adjust to the darkness. Still, they could barely see any stars. The trees effectively covered everything up except for the occasional brighter star that appeared through the trees. A light breeze blew the branches high above, adding an additional twinkle to the occasional visible star.

The group walked in a straight line. The counselor led the walk, and everyone followed slowly behind him, each person putting his hands forward on the shoulders of the person in front of him. This technique made walking in the dark pretty easy.

After about ten minutes the path opened up into a large field. The contrast from the narrow dark path they had just left, to the star-lit field they suddenly entered, was stunning. Nothing could describe the impact of truly seeing the night sky for the first time far away from the light pollution of a town or city. Even Joshua, who had seen the stars like this his entire life, never ceased to be amazed.

The group made their way to the middle of the field, and the counselor began his talk. He started by pointing out the "Big Dipper." This constellation was always the easiest to learn, and usually the most recognizable, and so it provided an excellent reference point for learning the other constellations.

The counselor used its connecting stars as pointers to other less familiar constellations. Most of the kids were impressed as they gazed south to the end of the field and made out the image of a scorpion's pointed tail in one constellation. Of course, the Scouts only realized the resemblance to a scorpion after the counselor told them that it was one. In this respect, looking at constellations was much like trying to discover images in clouds. Everyone perceived something different but could easily see what the other person saw after it was described.

The Astronomy counselor only spent about twenty minutes pointing out stars and constellations. He knew from experience that the kid's attention spans wouldn't last much longer. The night sky had a tendency to grab one's imagination along with one's attention. The counselor learned to indulge the stream of consciousness that inevitably followed.

"Ask whatever catches your interest," he said, as he ended his formal lecture. He had done this enough times to anticipate the inevitable first question. No matter how many times he led a hike, he was amazed at how many times one particular question always came up. He couldn't help but laugh every time it did.

It was Nick who asked the question this time. "What's that star up there called?" Nick asked in amazement, as he pointed to a star in the sky. Of course, Nick knew exactly which star he meant, but no one else could possibly make out which one his finger was pointing to.

Other questions soon followed.

"Is there life out there?" a boy from another troop asked. This was another question that was typically asked. The counselor enjoyed answering this one. Kids liked speculating about life on other planets and what it must be like up in space. But the counselor didn't get a chance to answer. He could no longer ignore the sighs of amazement he heard from a few of the Scouts behind him. Others had already turned around as they heard the sighs.

CHAPTER SIX

"What are they looking at?" the counselor wondered almost angrily, as he turned around. The answer was immediately apparent. No one needed to point it out. It was not a star.

A curtain of blue-green lights shimmered from the horizon upward in waves, extending apparently endlessly into infinity. The counselor dropped the flashlight he had been using to point out stars with.

"My God," the counselor said in quiet amazement. "Enjoy this while you can," he said to the Scouts. "It's a once in a lifetime experience."

"What is it?" one boy asked quietly, unable to take his eyes off it.

"The Northern Lights," the counselor responded, also hypnotized by the scene.

The counselor had never actually seen them before. This phenomenon followed a few days after sun spot activity. If you happened to be in a field at night away from the city at the right time, one could witness it.

Even Joshua had never witnessed it before. He couldn't believe he was seeing it now. Everyone simply gazed at the lights, some literally with their mouths hung open.

Nick let his legs collapse underneath him and fell to the ground, propping up his body with his elbows. It was a much more comfortable way of viewing the phenomena. Most of the other kids followed. No one asked any more questions. They just watched in amazement.

Joshua and Cody stood behind everyone in the back. Cody's thoughts drifted for a second to Josh, who was standing next to him. He was glad to be experiencing this event with Joshua. Cody put his hand around Joshua's shoulder. They watched the sky and enjoyed it together.

A SCOUT IS BRAVE

*****

Josh and his friends talked only about the Northern Lights as they made their way back to camp following the hike. It was almost midnight by the time they reached main camp. The counselor had intended to have everyone back much earlier, but he was not about to deny them the experience of the Aurora Borealis.

He wished them a good night as they all broke off into separate groups and headed back to their campsites. At the corner of his eyes, Joshua caught a glimpse of Tommy's Point on the other side of the lake, as the light of the rising moon reflected off of it. Joshua had completely forgotten about Tommy Drapos up until then. What a shame, Joshua thought to himself, that Tommy didn't have friends like the ones he had.

Everything was quiet as Joshua entered the campsite with his friends. The other Scouts in their troop had gone to bed and fallen asleep hours ago. The first day's activities had worn everyone out.

Joshua was once again the last person to enter the tent after the trip to the sink. Again, Robby was already fast asleep in just the few minutes it took Josh to brush. Joshua noticed that Robby wore a sweater this time. It didn't take long for the new Scouts to realize that Wisconsin nights got a lot colder than Illinois nights.

Joshua pulled off his pants and slipped into his sleeping bag next to Cody. "Goodnight Cody," he whispered, not wanting to awaken Robby, assuming that was even possible.

"Goodnight, Red Feather," Cody responded. "Thanks," he added, whispering gently.

CHAPTER SIX

Joshua was confused by that response. "Thanks for what?" he inquired back.

"I don't know," Cody said. "Just everything I guess. You know?"

Cody couldn't clarify his feelings any further, but he didn't have to. Joshua knew exactly what he meant. Just knowing that someone else was out there who was like him, just being able to talk about it, was quite cathartic.

"You're welcome," Joshua answered.

The image of Tommy's Point shimmering in the moonlight invaded Josh's thoughts. He remembered his dream from the night before. Poor Tommy, Joshua thought to himself once again before drifting off to sleep.

*****

A brilliant and terrifying flash of lightning revealed a vulnerable Tommy Drapos standing naked. The fellow Scouts stood around him laughing furiously. Blood was dripping from his behind, where he had been violated. The pain he felt from the stick was nothing compared to the humiliation. Every laugh from his tormentors was like a dagger in his back. He couldn't hold back the tears, and that only made his tormentors laugh harder.

Finally, Tommy couldn't take it anymore. He stood up and ran as fast as he could into the dark woods. His bare feet hurt as they impacted with the sticks and rocks that paved the forest floor. But Tommy didn't care. All he wanted was to get away from the taunts that were coming from behind him. No matter how hard he ran, the laughter never stopped. It seemed to follow him, to close in on him, even though he knew that the boys were no longer there.

The laughter was all around him. Tommy couldn't get his bearings. He stopped and looked around frantically. There was no one there, yet the laughter continued. He didn't know where he was. He was cold, naked, and lost. Rain smashed into the ground, seemingly louder than the thunder.

"You better run, you faggot!" a strange voice warned. "I'm right behind you."

Tommy ran again, but he didn't know to where. He was gripped with fear and paid no attention to where he was going. He heard the footsteps behind him. No matter how fast he ran, they kept up. Sometimes it sounded like there were thousands of them. Other times only one or two.

"Better run faster, faggot; I'm right on top of you," the voice whispered seemingly right behind him.

Suddenly a sharp pain shot through his legs, as what felt like nails penetrated his thighs, ripping open his flesh. Tommy stumbled to the ground, shrieking in pain. A shock of recognition gripped his face as he caught a glimpse of what was chasing him. He stared directly into the face of the Beast and screamed as it closed on him. His legs reeled with pain as he got back up and ran.

Joshua observed everything. He desperately tried to focus on the face of the Demon. But it was all a blur. He couldn't make out anything.

Tommy stood up and ran once again, despite the pain that multiplied every time he put one step forward. He soon realized that running was hopeless as he emerged from the forest only to discover there was no where else to run. All he saw was the edge of a cliff and a lake thirty feet or so below him. He was trapped, and the Creature was closing.

Tommy reeled in pain as another gash sliced into his back. The pain was overwhelming, and Tommy lost his balance. He fell forward in slow motion and smashed into the rocks below. His body just laid there, mangled, naked, and dead.

Joshua heard the laughter everywhere now. He still couldn't make out the face of the Demon which had just pushed Tommy off the cliff. But the Creature was still there, and Joshua knew it was looking at him now.

He woke up in a cold sweat and let out a scream.

"Are you all right?" Cody and Robby both asked, as they jolted to awareness. Joshua caught his breath.

"Just a dream," he whimpered in response. "A very bad dream."

CHAPTER 7

Joshua didn't sleep well for the rest of the night. He got up early the next morning and hiked down to the lake. No one was up at 5:00 a.m. Camp seemed like an entirely different place, even main camp, which was typically bustling with activity. A silent mist quietly rolled off the water as the sun rose. Cody didn't join Joshua this time. He didn't even rouse when Joshua unzipped the tent flap. He was too tired from the night before.

Joshua sat down at the beach and stared across the lake. The mist was beautiful, and the lake was awake with wildlife. Fish punctured holes in the lake ceiling, grabbing at the insects crawling across its otherwise calm surface. Ducks and geese honked, and quacked, and played, and fought, oblivious to their surroundings. Hawks flew over head serenely taking in the activity below. Deer drank from the shore, enjoying the break from raucous Scouts.

Wildlife, it seemed, had reclaimed its home, if only for the early morning hours. But Joshua ignored all of this. All he could focus on was Tommy's Point. It absorbed his attention. That poor, lonely kid, Joshua thought, over and over again, fixating on the legend, and on his nightmare.

Joshua remained quiet most of the morning, even when the other Scouts finally awoke. Breakfast came and went, and morning badges passed quickly. Simply being around Cody helped Joshua make it through the day. Josh's group skipped Citizenship merit badge, just as they planned, and hung out at the Trading Post instead. They had Cody to thank for that one.

Indian Lore merit badge proved interesting. They learned how to weave Indian baskets and make beaded bracelets and necklaces. Joshua and Cody made one for each other.

"Friends forever," Cody said, as he tied his bracelet around Joshua's arm.

"Friends forever," Joshua agreed, returning the gesture.

After lunch, the boys waited for Joshua at the benches in front of the Dining Hall. Joshua was waiter that period and so was a bit late in arriving. They sat down and reviewed their plans for the afternoon.

Pastor Bob also sat down at the benches. He was talking to some of the Scoutmasters from the other troops. Cody soon realized that they were discussing homosexuality.

Pastor Bob was giving them a preview of the sermon he was going to perform for his troop later that night. He delivered one to the boys every couple of days and was very proud of them. Naturally, he had to make sure that other Scoutmasters heard his sermons as well.

Part of his speech was about sexuality. This is how homosexuality came up. Pastor Bob could barely finish the word "gay," without falling into a diatribe about how it was a perverted "lifestyle choice."

"How could anyone choose such a thing?" Pastor Bob rhetorically asked in a disgusted tone. "To choose such a thing is the gravest of sins against our Lord and against nature," he continued. The other Scoutmasters were typically annoyed at Pastor Bob's constant preaching. But on this subject they all seemed to agree, and his captive audience nodded accordingly.

Cody didn't mean to intrude on the conversation, but he felt he had to say something. "How could you choose to be attracted to someone?" Cody asked innocently. "Aren't you just born that way?" he offered.

A bomb seemingly exploded. Cody's friends were standing nearby. Their own conversations came to a sudden stop. They wanted to save the life of their best friend, but he had just sealed his own doom. They just stood there, mouths agape, waiting for Pastor Bob to execute Cody right in front of them.

"Excuse me for a second," Pastor Bob said to the other Scoutmasters. His face betrayed a sense of shock and humiliation.

"Son, I need to talk to you for a second. Go over there, and I'll be right with you." He pointed towards the trail that headed back to their campsite.

Cody realized that he had made a big mistake. But somehow it just seemed easier to talk about homosexuality now that he had already spent a few hours discussing it with Joshua. Taboo subjects rarely seem forbidden once shared. And frankly Cody didn't think he had said anything to his father that was out of line. The sight of Pastor Bob coming toward him with an angry look on his face dramatically illustrated otherwise.

Pastor Bob grabbed and pinched his son's ear as he caught up with him.

"Come with me," he grunted, pulling his son forward.

"Ouch," Cody whimpered, as his dad pulled him down the trail.

"Dad, that hurts!" he cried out.

"Don't you ever embarrass me like that again in front of anyone!" Pastor Bob shouted. He didn't let go of his son's ear, as he continued his tirade. "What's the matter with you anyway? Do you want people to think you are some sort of queer!" Pastor Bob got a sick look on his face as he said that word.

"Now get back to camp!" he yelled, letting go of Cody's ear. Cody ran down the trail back to the campsite. He cried all the way back.

*****

Joshua unzipped his tent flap and crawled in. He was panting hard, as he had run all the way from the Dining Hall as soon as his friends informed him of the exchange between Cody and his father.

Cody lay on his sleeping bag facing the tent roof apparently lost in thought. Joshua could tell he had been crying since tears were still running down his cheeks.

"I hate him," Cody said, his voice cracking. Tears started to form in his eyes again.

Cody had always felt this way about his father. Pastor Bob was a respected member of their community back at home, with his reputation as a man of God and all. But Cody lived with him. If Pastor Bob was a man of God, Cody felt, then Cody wanted nothing to do with God.

Pastor Bob always emphasized discipline and respect for one's elders. Cody came to the conclusion long ago that respect had to be earned. But whatever Cody's feeling were in the past, they were multiplied a thousand fold by this recent incident. Cody simply gave his opinion on a subject that he knew far more about than his father ever could. His father had treated him with contempt.

"I wish he were dead," Cody admitted. He began to cry again.

"Cody, it'll be alright," Josh said, trying to comfort his friend. Joshua sat down next to him. He didn't really know what else to say. Before he knew it, he was telling Cody about his parents.

"My parents sometimes think I'm possessed by Satan," Joshua offered. It was a deadpan delivery.

Cody looked at him. For a second he wasn't sure if Joshua was kidding. All his anger and hatred was replaced by an irresistible urge to laugh. He couldn't hold it anymore, and soon he was chuckling so hard he started crying again. Joshua joined in the laughter, although he wasn't entirely sure that he had been kidding.

Josh's mom really wondered about Joshua sometimes. She staunchly disapproved of his interest in Indian traditions. Her religion preached the supremacy of their "One and true Lord and Savior, Jesus Christ." Native American spirituality seemed to her like some sort of barbaric pagan religion, possibly even Satanic.

The only reason she sent Joshua to camp was so he could be influenced by true religion. But it wasn't much of a religion, Joshua thought to himself, pondering the way Pastor Bob treated his son.

"Come on," Joshua called, as he got up and started to leave the tent. "Let's go sacrifice animals to Satan or something," he teased.

Cody wiped his tears and followed Joshua, still laughing. Seconds ago he was so angry and hurt that he wanted his father dead. But now all he could do was laugh. Joshua made Cody feel a joy for life that he had never felt before. Only a twisted and perverted mind, Cody realized, would consider such joy a sin. Cody was determined from that point on to enjoy his time together with Joshua. No one else mattered, least of all his father.

*****

Joshua and Cody initially planned to do some more observations for their Environmental Science merit badge, but neither were really in the mood. The notes didn't really matter anyway. Thanks to Joshua, in only two hours the boys had collected enough information to write their report. They could simply make it seem like they collected their material during the course of the week. That was more than anyone else had done.

They still had two hours to kill before they met up with their friends again for swimming. No matter, as they enjoyed simply talking with each other. They got so immersed in conversation that they failed to pay attention to where they were headed. By the time they realized it, the two boys had reached a restricted area.

There were only a few areas in camp designated as "Off Limits." Some of these areas, like Tommy's Point, were labeled as such for safety reasons. Other areas were set aside to provide camp staff members with some breathing space, a sort of sanctuary from the Scouts.

Most of the staff enjoyed working with kids, otherwise they wouldn't have taken the job. But even the most devoted staff member needed the occasional quiet time, undisturbed by the "demonic bundles of energy," as one counselor jokingly put it. Camp staff worked all day, and many of them, deep into the night. Respite time was absolutely essential.

Josh and Cody realized they had wandered into one of these staff areas. It was dotted with small cabins where the staff had their quarters. One building stood out for its size. Through its screen windows, Joshua could make out ping-pong tables and a soda pop machine. This was the staff lounge, they realized.

"We better get out of here," Cody whispered.

"Yeah," agreed Joshua, as they turned around and started back down the trail.

As they turned around, they heard whispering coming from the woods surrounding the staff area. Through the brush, Joshua and Cody recognized Jim Meeder, their former Citizenship merit badge counselor. He was with someone else, but they couldn't tell who. Then they realized it was one of the Aquatics instructors.

Joshua and Cody knew they had to leave before these two spotted them. Joshua especially wanted to avoid getting in trouble with Jim Meeder again. But they both froze as they witnessed something quite unexpected. They watched as Jim Meeder embraced the other counselor and kissed him. The counselors were oblivious to the fact that two very astonished Scouts stood frozen nearby. Like the proverbial deer in the headlights, Josh and Cody simply stared at the impossible scene.

"Oh my God!" Cody said much louder than he had intended, finally breaking the spell.

Jim and the other counselor immediately spotted them. Jim recognized Joshua and Cody right away. The counselor's faces turned red, and their minds raced for an excuse to explain their predicament.

Joshua's anxiety immediately subsided as he realized that it was the counselors who were frightened. Jim Meeder wouldn't turn them in for trespassing, not when the Scouts had witnessed an even greater transgression. But Joshua was not about to take advantage of the situation.

"Sorry, we didn't mean to disturb you," Joshua said, grabbing Cody by the arm and quickly walking down the path away from the staff area.

The two staff members were still partially in shock. That was the last reaction they expected to get from two young Scouts. "Faggot," maybe, but not "sorry to disturb you." As soon as Meeder regained his composure, he ran after Joshua.

"Wait a second," he called to them from behind.

Joshua and Cody stopped to let Jim catch up. When he did, they continued walking. Jim sounded very nervous. His face was still red, and sweat poured down his face.

"Let me explain," he pleaded.

"What's to explain?" Joshua responded.

"Yeah," said Cody. "No big deal."

But Joshua decided not to leave it at that. He had a score to settle with Jim. He still hadn't gotten over being so cavalierly dismissed by Jim the previous day.

"Just tell me something," Joshua said, "How can you love a country so greatly that hates you so much?"

Jim was obviously stunned, and his face betrayed near panic. Jim simply couldn't believe he was having this conversation, openly discussing his sexual orientation. It was difficult to get used to.

But Jim felt like he had to discuss it. Joshua had caught him red-handed. Who knew what this young Scout would say to others? Everyone at camp would know that he and his friend were gay. They would be fired, or maybe something much worse. This had to be dealt with now.

"We can't hold people accountable for following what their religion teaches them," Jim responded, thinking he had just made perfect sense.

"I think we can hold them responsible for plenty," Joshua quickly retorted.

Jim stopped following the two boys as they started to veer off onto another path. He just stood their, wondering what to do next.

"You're not going to tell anyone about what you saw?" Jim finally asked, seemingly on the verge of panic.

"Who would care?" Joshua called back. "It's a free country, right?" Josh said, as he continued walking.

Jim Meeder didn't miss the sarcasm in that response. It was quite biting.

*****

Joshua and Cody couldn't really discuss what they had just witnessed. They had reached main camp, and there were too many people around. Instead, they talked more about their Environmental Science report, as they headed towards the showers. Neither of them had washed that morning. Cody woke up too late, and Joshua simply hadn't felt like showering so early. But as the hours passed, the heat had gotten to them, and they were starting to smell from hiking and sweating all day.

The showers were empty when they arrived. Normally, they were busiest in the morning before breakfast and in the evening after dinner. Throughout most of the afternoon, on the other hand, one could reasonably count on sparse attendance; hence, warm water.

Joshua began to undress first. He yanked his shirt off and threw it on the ground. He noticed that Cody wasn't as fast at undressing as he had been in their tent the day they met. Cody started with his shoes and socks and then stalled before moving onto his shirt and pants.

Joshua knew exactly why. He felt the same way. They were both a little self-conscious now that they knew the others' sexual orientation. Getting undressed in front of each other suddenly felt awkward. Joshua decided simply to ignore it. Eventually they would get used to it, he felt.

The shower water felt perfect. Joshua had already drenched his long, black hair by the time Cody walked in. Cody also seemed intent to ignore the awkwardness. He promptly turned on a shower and began to wash. They both averted their eyes, anxious not to appear curious.

The initial discomfort soon passed as the water washed away their anxiety. Cody broke the ice first by bringing up the upcoming "Order of the Arrow" ceremony, something he felt Joshua would be especially interested in. The Order, or OA, as it was called, was an organization within Scouting dedicated to preserving Native American traditions. They would be putting on a ceremony on Wednesday night for the entire camp. Cody told Josh all about it. He had seen the ceremony several times before during previous summers. Josh had no idea that they did anything like that in Scouting, and he was excited to see the program. Between Environmental Science, Indian Lore, and now the Order of the Arrow, Joshua was really starting to enjoy Scouting. It was not what he had expected. Perhaps his mother was right to get him involved, Josh thought.

The two finished washing, turned off the water, and walked over to their clothes. They were both a lot less self-conscious now. Just before leaving the shower area, they heard voices from the locker room. They tensed up once again as they recognized the voices.

Levi walked into the shower area still laughing from a joke one of his friends just told. He seemed just as surprised to see Joshua and Cody as they were to see him. But it wasn't Levi who had been literally caught with his pants down.

"Well, if it isn't Red Feather," Levi said, "the guy who wants to be my," he paused before finishing in an effeminate tone, "friend." He let his hand fall limp imitating a stereotypical gay male. Levi's entourage walked in behind him just in time to join in.

"Cover yourself up guys," Levi said to his friends. "You never know who is watching." His friends put their hands over their genitals, playing along with their leader.

"So, is this where your kind hangs out?" Levi asked, staring directly into Joshua's eyes.

Joshua and Cody quickly finished dressing and headed towards Levi, who was blocking their exit. The two boys simply stepped around him without flinching.

"What are you looking at?" Ken Fenton asked, looking at Joshua accusingly, as Josh tried to leave. The implication was clear. He had subtly accused Joshua of visually groping him. This was a bully tactic that only the most talented and skilled could pull off. Ken thought this was the perfect opportunity to regain face with his friends. Joshua and Cody were doomed.

Unscathed, Joshua stopped, faced Ken directly, and then glanced down for a second. He then looked back up in Ken's eyes, put his hand on Ken's shoulder in sympathy, and responded, "Apparently nothing much." The other boys broke out in hysterical laughter. Only then did Ken realize that he had been verbally emasculated. Joshua and Cody made their getaway in the confusion. Even Levi was too busy laughing to notice that his two victims had just given him the slip.

*****

Joshua and Cody spent the rest of the afternoon swimming in the lake with their friends. It was a pleasant refuge now that Levi had been evicted from the area. The boys could now concentrate on their game of tag without harassment.

As before, Robby dominated the game. By now it was pretty obvious to the group that Robby wanted to be it. No one, they knew, could accidentally get tagged that many times. But they didn't care. It was still fun.

Robby shot forward towards Joshua, but Joshua quickly ducked down under water and slipped away. Joshua wasn't the fastest swimmer above the water, but underneath, no one could beat him. He plunged up for air after swimming about thirty feet. He looked around, and sure enough, Robby had given up pursuit.

Joshua relaxed a bit, but he didn't let down his guard. For all he knew, someone else could have been tagged while he was under the water. So, anyone around him could be "it." Then he saw Robby dart after Cody, betraying the fact that Robby was still it.

Unexpectedly, Joshua noticed one of the lifeguards staring at him. The staffmember had an anxious look on his face, as though he had just been caught committing a crime. Josh thought this was strange at first, but then he recognized the guy. It was the counselor that he had caught with Jim Meeder in the staff area. The lifeguard seemed extremely apprehensive, as if everyone was glaring at him. He obviously didn't know yet how lucky he had been. Of all the people that could have caught him with Jim Meeder, it turned out to be two gay Scouts.

Joshua was glad that he discovered the two of them. It felt comforting to know that he wasn't the only gay person in the world, just as when he learned about Cody. Looking around, Joshua now realized that there were probably lots of gay people out there, just blending in like everyone else. He had never truly been alone.

*****

Swim time flew by quickly, and soon the Scouts had to leave to get ready for dinner. Josh and Cody wanted to get back to the beach as soon as possible. Dinner couldn't end fast enough. They decided that aquatic activities suited them best. As long as the beach was off-limits to Levi, that's where they wanted to be.

Fortunately, the Aquatics area staff announced that they were opening the boating area after dinner. Cody and Josh decided to go canoeing. Joshua had been wanting to canoe ever since he arrived at camp, but afternoon boating time had always conflicted with his other badges. The evening was the only time he and Cody could do it. They both finished their food quickly and restlessly waited for supper to end.

The two then noticed Pastor Bob get up and say something to each of the tables occupied by his Scouts. He finally made his way over to their table. The boys pretended to give Pastor Bob their undivided attention.

"Don't forget my church service after dinner tonight," he reminded everyone. It'll be at our campsite," he said, quickly moving on to the next table. "Mandatory," he announced as he looked back at them.

"Damn!" Joshua said after Pastor Bob had left. The church service had completely slipped their minds. Given the fact that Cody was Pastor Bob's son, there was no hope of skipping out without being noticed.

"Don't worry," Cody said. "It shouldn't last long. We should be able to catch some of the canoeing time after his sermon is over."

This was of little comfort to Joshua, but it was better than nothing.

Most of the troop was sitting around the campfire by the time Joshua and Cody arrived. Pastor Bob was going over some notes as though this was going to be the most important speech of his life. Most of his audience just wanted him to get started and get it over with. When Pastor Bob finally got his notes in order, he looked up at his Scouts with a very stern expression.

"Reverence is one of the most important points in the Scout law," he began, repeating the lines exactly as he had practiced many times. "Respect for God is essential to the development of any good citizen. Thus, we will have these services regularly throughout the week."

Pastor Bob waved his hand, and two boys dutifully got up and read a selection from the Bible. No one really listened or cared, but judging from their faces every Scout seemed to be listening with intense respect and interest. It didn't take long for Boy Scouts to master this skill, especially in Pastor Bob's troop. Whatever the Scouts really thought of his oration, they were wise enough to put up the pretense of respect.

After the reading, another boy led them in a few hymns. Pastor Bob shared one thing in common with his Scouts. He eagerly wanted all these formalities to end, but for different reasons. Pastor Bob wanted to deliver his sermon; the boys just wanted to leave.

Finally, the singing ended and Pastor Bob began his sermon. He got up before them, and stared intently at his notes. "I want to discuss something important with you," he said. "Something that I know a lot of you are probably starting to have questions about." His tone was deeply serious. "You are reaching that age when the body undergoes certain changes, changes that will make you have certain urges that you have never had before."

"Oh my God," the boys in the troop simultaneously realized, Pastor Bob was going to talk about sex.

"Just please kill me now," Cody whispered to Joshua, unable to contain his embarrassment. Joshua patted his back.

The campers all wondered why Pastor Bob didn't just say it. Adults had a tendency to use every word in the dictionary except the one that everyone understood, especially when discussing uncomfortable subjects.

"Now, what you have to understand," Pastor Bob continued, "is that these urges are a test from God. God wants you to love him with all your body and soul. In order to do this you will have to discipline these urges."

The kids knew he was now going to tell them how.

"The Bible specifically says that the only proper outlet for these urges is in the context of marriage. Now, you will all grow up and eventually get girlfriends. But let me tell you that as much as you are tempted, you must show that your love for God is stronger and wait until marriage."

The kids were amazed. Pastor Bob had nearly completed an entire sermon on sex without mentioning the word at all. He was truly skilled.

CHAPTER SEVEN

Suddenly, Pastor Bob's tone darkened.

"Now, given these new urges you will be feeling, many of you will get confused. You will not know how to respond to your body's 'needs.' This is when Satan will try to take advantage of you. This is when he will tempt you to pervert those urges into something debased. This is what leads to homosexuality, bestiality, and pedophilia," Pastor Bob said, as if they were all the same thing. The Scouts had no idea what bestiality and pedophilia were, but they knew about homosexuality.

Levi had been staring off into space throughout most of the lecture. Like most of the Scouts he simply wanted to get out of there. But suddenly he seemed to take interest. Joshua and Cody took an interest also.

"All I'm saying is that you have choices," the Pastor attempted to clarify.

"You can choose God, and live a happy, productive life, with the knowledge that you are doing God's will." He paused for a second and then continued. "Or, you can choose the perverted lifestyle of homosexuality." He fixed his gaze on Cody at this point, indicating his dismissal of Cody's earlier argument.

Joshua sat next to Cody and looked as though he was about to shout something out and interrupt Pastor Bob, just like he had interrupted Jim Meeder's lecture earlier in the week. Cody noticed this and put his hand on Josh's shoulder with a worried look.

Levi noticed these actions. He had noticed a lot of things about Joshua in the past couple of days.

"It is your choice," Pastor Bob declared, bringing his sermon to a close. "God bless you all." Before he could finish that last sentence, his Scouts had already begun to get up and leave.

Joshua and Cody got up and gathered with Timmy, Robby, and Nick. They quickly collected their stuff and headed off for the beach. But Joshua never lost the angered expression on his face. Levi observed Joshua carefully, watching him head down the trail away from the campsite with his friends.

*****

Josh and friends had missed about an hour of canoeing by the time they arrived at the beach. The lake was dotted with canoes and rowboats. Several canoes were still left on the shore, enough for all of them. Cody and Joshua shared one of the canoes, while Robby, Timmy, and Nick tripled up and took another.

The boys crawled into their canoes and paddled their way to the middle of the lake where the other Scouts had congregated. One of the Aquatics staff was giving instructions to the surrounding Scouts, while two other lifeguards circled the group and patrolled. Joshua and his friends arrived just in time to get in on the fun. Evidently they were all getting ready to "swamp" their canoes. Everyone had life jackets on, so it was perfectly safe. Just the same, the lifeguards gave an endless list of rules to ensure perfect security.

"All right, swamp your canoes!" the lifeguard shouted after finishing his speech.

In a matter of seconds, canoes were tipping over and the boys were splashing in the cool lake water. It had been an extremely hot day, and the lake water was intensely satisfying. The lifeguard would let them splatter around for twenty minutes or so before directing them back. They would have to swim back while dragging their canoes behind them, since they were filled with water. Some of the more experienced Scouts had learned how to empty the water from a canoe while it was in the lake. But that defeated the purpose of this evening. They were there to get wet and stay wet.

Water drenched Joshua's hair as Cody splashed him frantically from behind. Joshua quickly returned the favor. Meanwhile, Robby snuck around Joshua from the other end, catching Joshua off guard. Now Joshua was getting it from both directions.

Power shifts occurred frequently in this game, however, and soon Robby swung his attention around just in time to stave off a concerted attack from both Nick and Timmy. Joshua laughed hysterically as the two drenched Robby unexpectedly from behind. Cody broke off his attack on Joshua and joined in on the attack against Robby.

Joshua watched intently, using the brief moment of relaxation to decide who to get next. As he thought about it, a sight caught his eye in the distance. The sun was beginning to set at the other end of the lake leaving a beautiful silhouette image of Tommy's Point. Joshua filed the image in his mental buffer, as he noticed Robby and Cody trying to outflank him again.

The aquatic revelry seemed to last for hours. But they were out of there by 9:00 p.m. The sun was starting to set. Everyone was drenched. Cody and Josh walked back to their campsite slowly, hoping to dry off on the way back.

They were both exhausted when they arrived back at their campsite. Joshua had always been the last to get back to the tent and to sleep, but the past couple of days had taken its toll on him. He hadn't slept well since they arrived, thanks to his nightmares. Joshua skipped brushing altogether, and collapsed on his sleeping bag. The last thing he remembered before falling asleep was Robby and Cody filing into the tent. Joshua was dimly aware of them, as they wished him a goodnight.

*****

The lightening and thunder was furious, seemingly alive with rage. Rain pounded onto the forest below with extreme violence, echoing the rage. Powerful flashes of lightening illuminated Tommy Drapos' cold, mangled body as it rested on the rocks by the lake. Blood poured from his head onto the beach and into the restless water. The lightening was almost blinding now, and the thunder was so loud it seemed like it would burst Josh's eardrums.

Despite its thunderous roar, it didn't mask all of the sounds. Joshua made out a noise even more prominent than the thunder. But he couldn't localize it; it radiated from all directions. It was the sound of kids laughing at the mangled body of Tommy Drapos.

Suddenly the sound localized itself around a dark manifestation stationed menacingly at the top of Tommy's Point. Joshua stared at the Demon in disbelief. Its dark form seemed unaffected by the lightening blasts that illuminated its surroundings. The Creature somehow managed to retain its pure darkness.

The laughter never stopped. Joshua took one last stare at Tommy's body, and the full impact of this cruel murder finally hit him. The slaying of Tommy Drapos was utterly cold and senseless. Tears poured down Joshua's eyes as an empty sadness gripped him. But as he stared at the Beast, the sadness transformed into an intense rage.

114

CHAPTER SEVEN

"You bastard!" Joshua shouted at the top of his lungs, challenging the monster.

Joshua could barely hear himself scream over the deafening sounds of thunder. No one heard his voice. For a second, he wasn't even sure if he had screamed. The thunder and laughter masked his voice so completely. Yet somehow the Creature had heard him and the laughter stopped. Joshua saw the dark shadowy figure turn and look towards him.

Fear suddenly gripped Joshua. He was alone in the middle of the woods, the sole witness to a callous murder. The slayer was staring right at him.

Joshua turned and ran as fast as he could. His feet pounded into the mud, making his steps awkward and unstable. Drenched leaves from the branches painfully whipped his face as he ran through the forest. Behind him he could hear the deafening footsteps of an enormous mass moving quickly behind him. Again the laughter resonated.

"Joshua," the Demon called out from somewhere close behind him. "Where are you going Joshua?" The voice was soulless.

Joshua didn't have an answer. He just ran as fast as he could, hoping somehow to lose the threatening figment. But he didn't. It kept up with him with every desperate step he made.

"You can't get away, Joshua. I'm everywhere." The dark figure repeated this last sentence over and over. It echoed through Joshua's head until Josh could no longer think.

"Everywhere!"

Joshua lost his footing and slipped. He smashed into the ground as he completely lost control. His hands were impaled by some branches lying on the ground, and his chest impacted with some rocks. He could barely breath as he lay there grasping for air. Rain pelted him like rocks.

Suddenly, everything went silent; no voices, no laughter, no thunder. Joshua looked around frantically for the Demon but saw nothing. Then, abruptly, a large dark mass walked closely towards him, standing only a few feet away.

Joshua's eyes widened as he gazed directly into the face of the Demon that had been chasing him, into the malevolent Spirit that had exterminated Tommy Drapos. For an instant he thought he recognized it. Then its face blurred, and Joshua awoke from his nightmare.

The blurred image of the devil's face dominated his thoughts, even as the dream world was replaced by reality. He was certain that he had recognized that face.

CHAPTER 8

Joshua and Cody loitered at the Trading Post after breakfast the next morning. It was a good place to work on their Indian baskets for Indian Lore merit badge while killing time before Environmental Science at 10:00 a.m. The task of weaving the basket was easy, but monotonous.

Joshua hadn't told Cody about the nightmares he had been having. He knew that Cody was spooked about Tommy Drapos, and Josh didn't want to make things any worse. But Cody knew something was wrong with Joshua since Josh had woken up in a cold sweat twice that week and slept restlessly throughout the night.

Attendance at the Trading Post was sparse as usual right after breakfast. The counselor running the Trading Post was glad for the company. He came out and talked to Cody and Joshua for awhile, as the two worked on their baskets.

Joshua soon finished his and began to mentally review the other tasks he still had to complete. It was then that he realized he left his Environmental Science notebook back in his tent. The Scouts were supposed to discuss their observations today in class. Joshua needed his notebook for that. He told Cody he would be right back and dashed to his campsite to get it.

Cody would have followed, but he needed to finish his basket. Also, he had already purchased a soda, and food and drink were only allowed in the Trading Post area. That rule managed to keep the rest of camp relatively clean from snack-food debris.

It was no big deal, Cody thought, since Joshua would probably only be gone for a few minutes. But it was exactly the few minutes for which Levi had been waiting.

Levi had thought a lot about Joshua lately. It wasn't the usual vengeance kind of thinking. Levi had noticed that Joshua hadn't denied being gay, despite three separate intimations.

It did occur to Levi that rather than deny it and play right into Levi's hands, Joshua simply had the sense to ignore him. Levi knew by now that Joshua was smart enough to avoid his little traps.

But last night Levi saw how Joshua reacted to Pastor Bob's sermon. It didn't make sense. Something seemed odd about Joshua's apparent anxiety. Levi began to suspect that Joshua really was gay, but he had to find out for sure.

If it were true, then Levi could really have some fun. Beyond that, he was sickened by the thought that there might really be an actual queer in his troop. The thought bothered him even more when Levi realized that Joshua had bested him several times.

Cody saw Levi and his gang approaching from the Handicraft area. He thought nothing of it at first. Levi had done nothing all that bad since he dunked Robby on Monday. So, Cody let his guard down. He didn't even realize that Levi was heading right towards him. By the time he took notice, it was too late to do anything about it.

The Trading Post counselor had gone back inside to take inventory, and Joshua was probably already back at the campsite. Cody was all alone, but he kept his cool. Levi stepped in front of Cody as Levi's band circled around behind him.

Cody didn't know how he was going to respond. "No one's in the mood," Cody said in a tough tone. He surprised himself. Perhaps Joshua had rubbed off on him, he thought.

Levi ignored the tone. "Relax, I'm not here to pick on you. You'd probably just get us thrown out of the Trading Post anyway."

Cody was surprised by Levi's response. He knew immediately that he was serious. He acted as though he had something important to tell him.

"It's about your friend," Ken said, circling around behind Cody, as if interrogating him. "Pink Feather," or whatever you call him. The other boys laughed. Ken finally scored some points.

Levi motioned him to be quiet. Levi wanted complete charge of this conversation.

"We think he's a queer," Levi said with disgust in his mouth.

"Very funny," Cody said, hoping his shock didn't show. But he was nervous inside. His mind raced for some sort of explanation. How could Levi possibly know about Joshua? And if he knew about Joshua, did he know about him as well? Sweat formed on Cody's forehead as he contemplated that thought.

"This is no joke," Levi said seriously. His eyelids narrowed.

Cody knew he had to convince Levi that he was wrong. If it came out that he was gay, then his life was over. He could only imagine what his father would do.

He had heard his father talking about how gays could be "cured." It sounded like some sort of exorcism to him. Cody had to deny Levi's statements at all costs. "Evade" was the only word going through his mind.

"It's not true," Cody finally let out. He tried not to sound defensive. He figured the best approach was to keep his cool.

"Joshua is just different, that's all," Cody stated.

"Indians don't have hang-ups about sex like," he paused before finishing his sentence. "Like we do," he finally let out.

"That's why Josh got upset last night," Cody insisted. "That's all it is." Cody prayed that his explanation would be sufficient.

"No one is that different," Levi yelled, "unless they really are different." But Levi saw that he was getting nowhere, so he changed his tactic.

"It seems pretty strange that you are so defensive about this. Perhaps you have something to hide."

Of course, Cody had not appeared defensive at all. He kept his cool masterfully. Levi was merely attempting to thaw him out a bit.

"It seems to me that if there was a reason to believe my tentmate was a fag," Levi announced, "I would want to know for sure." Levi's friends all nodded in agreement. "I presume you will help us find out?"

"This is ridiculous," Cody jumped in. His discomfort was starting to show. "He's not gay!" Cody realized that he blurted that out a little too defensively, but it was too late to take it back.

"Fine, then he'll pass our test."

"What test?" Cody inquired hesitantly, not liking the sound of this.

"I want you to get Joshua alone somewhere and try to kiss him. If he lets you, then we'll know."

CHAPTER EIGHT

"You're crazy!" Cody accused. He tried to look disgusted by the suggestion. He stood up and tried to get around Levi so he could leave.

"I told you, it's not true," he insisted.

"Then he won't let you kiss him," Levi reasoned. "So what's the problem?"

"But then he'll think I'm gay," Cody protested, hoping to sound sincere.

"I thought you said he didn't have a problem with faggots?" Levi countered.

"My father does!" Cody protested.

"That didn't seem to bother you yesterday when you defended queers!" Levi screamed angrily.

Cody didn't know that Levi had heard about that. It was a small camp. Cody realized now what a mistake that exchange with his father had been. He didn't know what to say. Levi just wouldn't back down.

"I was just making a point," Cody said. He got up from the bench he was sitting on and tried to walk away. Levi blocked him. He stared deeply into Cody's eyes, like he was reading his soul. How does he do that? Cody wondered. Cody stepped around Levi, trying desperately to maintain his composure. This time Levi gave in. Cody headed toward the path back to camp. But he knew it wasn't over. Levi wasn't going to let this drop.

"It's for your own good," Levi yelled after him. "I'd want to know if there was a queer in the troop, especially if it was my best friend!"

Cody ignored him and just kept walking, but inside he was terrified. As he started up the trail, he noticed that his hands were trembling with fear.

*****

Cody began running as soon as he left Levi's sight. He collided with Joshua, who was walking back from the campsite with his notebook. Cody was out of breath and panting. He was gripped by fear and panic.

"What's wrong?" Joshua asked concerned. He was surprised to see Cody on the trail.

"They know," Cody said frantically, as he gulped down more air.

Joshua put his hands on Cody's shoulders. He gazed into Cody's eyes with a soothing expression. "Hold on a minute," Josh said, trying to calm his friend down. "Just relax." Joshua waited patiently as Cody caught his breath. "Now tell me what happened?"

"They know," Cody repeated. "Levi and his friends know that you're gay." Cody breathed in before continuing. "I told them it wasn't true, but they wouldn't believe me. My God, Red Feather, what are we going to do?"

The desperation in his voice was obvious. Cody was terrified that his father would discover his secret.

Joshua looked him in the eye. "Cody, don't worry," he said in a calm voice. Cody relaxed a bit. "They can't prove anything. No one would believe them anyway. Everyone knows they are out to get me."

Cody thought about it for a second and realized Joshua was right. Levi couldn't prove anything. It was all speculation.

"We just have to be careful," Joshua reassured him.

The two split off from the trail that led to main camp hoping to avoid Levi. The trail they took went straight to the Ecology area where they took Environmental Science merit badge.

CHAPTER EIGHT

Cody's fears were almost completely quelled by the time they arrived. Just being with Joshua made him believe that nothing could go wrong. Joshua was always so confident and sure of himself.

As soon as they arrived at their merit badge, the two sat down with the other Scouts and waited for it to begin. A counselor soon arrived and asked each Scout to discuss his observations. By the time they got around to Joshua, Cody had completely forgotten about the entire incident. It still consumed Levi, however, who was back at the Trading Post planning his next move.

*****

As the morning merit badges came to an end, Cody and Josh shot over to the Dining Hall to wait for lunch to begin. They were both starving. By the time lunch began, Cody had completely forgotten about his earlier incident with Levi. But Levi's presence at the table next to him rekindled the terrifying episode. Cody couldn't help but notice Levi staring at him periodically throughout lunch. Levi really knew how to psyche someone out. But Joshua's reassurances prevailed. Cody just ignored Levi and tried not to look back.

Nick and Timmy mentioned that they wouldn't have Rowing merit badge that afternoon as they usually did. The Rowing counselor had gotten ahead in class and decided to give everyone a day off. So the two asked if they could join Cody and Joshua on their nature observations. Cody happily said yes. He wanted as many people around as possible; safety in numbers, he thought to himself. He didn't want to get caught alone with Levi ever again.

However, by the time lunch ended, Cody and Josh both completely forgot that Robby, Nick, and Timmy were coming along. The two had gotten used to just slipping off into the woods after lunch. By the time Nick got done waitering, Cody and Joshua were long gone.

"Where are they?" Nick said, as he exited the Dining Hall.

Robby and Timmy were waiting for Nick at the benches.

"They must have forgotten," Timmy responded.

"That's okay," Robby jumped in, "I know where they go." They all got up and followed Robby towards the trail. Levi and his crew were watching, and they followed closely, but quietly, behind.

*****

Cody and Joshua sat down on a log facing the lake. This is where they had done most of their observations. The opening by the lake formed a perfect area for animals to come and drink. In the process, animals left their footprints in the cool mud. Joshua had already observed the tracks of raccoons, deer, mice, squirrels, and chipmunks.

"It's so quiet and peaceful here," Cody said, as he sat down.

"It reminds me a lot like home. I mean my real home before I moved," Joshua told Cody. "I used to run off into the forest, and I'd sit by the lake for hours."

"I thought my parents were bad," Cody said. "Is it that bad for you at home?" he asked.

"I don't think my parents really like me," Joshua acknowledged, staring into the lake.

"One time I spent the whole night in the forest. I was about eleven then. I was so scared when I walked back home in the morning. I thought my parents were going to kill me for being so late."

"What happened?" Cody asked. "What did they do?"

"Nothing," said Joshua, his voice beginning to crack. "They didn't even know I had been gone." Joshua looked down. He was obviously hurt, but he tried to hide it.

"I would have missed you," Cody said, putting his hand on Joshua's shoulder.

Joshua looked up at Cody. He'd never known anyone like him before. Cody made him feel important. Joshua enjoyed the attention he got from Cody and his new friends. Joshua had never been a hero before; it felt good.

Another more prominent emotion surfaced within Joshua as well. He felt a deep connection to Cody, which he slowly began to label as love. Josh had never been in love before, so he wasn't quite sure. But he knew that Cody was all he could think about lately.

Cody started to lean over towards Joshua. He had wanted to kiss him for some time. He had no idea what it would be like, but sometimes it was all he could think about. He had been too nervous to try it earlier. But not anymore. They had gotten to know each other very well. The couple both knew how they felt about each other.

Joshua noticed Cody lean towards him. He put his arm around Cody and met him half-way. Their lips touched. Cody felt a tingling all over. He felt like he had known Joshua forever. They both smiled and tried it again. But this time their lips didn't touch.

"Faggot!" a loud angry voice shouted from the woods. "I knew it!"

Joshua and Cody jumped to their feet and faced the shouts. But they knew who it was before they spotted any faces. Levi had a very distinct voice.

Cody's face turned bright red, and his hands began to shake once again. Joshua was shocked as well, but he kept his cool.

Levi and his gang walked out of the woods, followed by Robby, Timmy, and Nick. They all had stunned expressions on their faces. Levi and friends had caught up with Timmy, Robby and Nick on the trail. They told him to follow if they wanted to see something very interesting. The boys figured it was some sort of trick but were too afraid to leave. It was no trick. What they just witnessed was very interesting.

Levi approached Joshua. "Well, it looks like Indian Boy is really Queer Boy!" he shouted out loud, before stopping in front of Joshua. Ken wasn't impressed. He thought "Pink Feather" was a better insult, but he didn't challenge Levi.

Cody had never felt so embarrassed in all his life. He had been caught red handed. There was no way to get out of this. How could one deny being gay after being caught kissing another boy?

In a split second, Cody processed all the possible reactions from his father. None of them were even remotely bearable. The likeliest outcome after Levi had beat the hell out of him, Cody figured, was that his father would kill him. Even if Pastor Bob didn't kill him, Cody knew his father would never let him see Joshua again.

Levi stared intently into Cody's eyes. Cody tensed up. It was all over now, Cody realized.

"Nice job, Cody," Levi said in a soothing and sincere tone. "I have to admit, I didn't think you were going to go through with it."

CHAPTER EIGHT

Cody was stunned for a second before realizing what this meant. Levi thought that Cody was doing the test after all. They still believed that Cody was straight.

"What?" Joshua asked confused.

"Shut up, Queer Boy," Levi shouted, as his friends broke out in laughter.

"Don't worry," Levi said to Timmy, Robby, and Nick. "Cody and I set this all up. We know how to catch a queer. Right, Cody?"

Cody said nothing. Sweat poured from his forehead. Joshua looked at him in disbelief. He knew how Cody felt about him. It was just another one of Levi's tricks, he believed.

"Right, Cody?" Levi repeated.

Cody looked away from Joshua. He saw Timmy, Robby, and Nick gazing at him, waiting for a response. Levi looked at Cody as well. The faces blurred and for a second all Cody could see was his father's face condemning him to hell.

"Right," Cody finally confirmed, as a tear welled up in his eye. He said it almost automatically. It was so easy. It just slipped out of his mouth. Just as quickly, he was cleared of all charges. He was free. How could anyone reject such an offer?

Joshua just peered at Cody, waiting for some sort of explanation or some sign that this wasn't really happening. But it never came. Cody wouldn't even look at him.

"Poor Queer Feather; he lost his boyfriend," Levi teased.

Joshua looked to Cody desperately. He still believed that Cody would say it wasn't true, that it wasn't a test. But Cody just stood there gazing down at the ground, as Levi and his friends had their fun. Cody had betrayed him. It had all been a lie since the very beginning. Joshua felt ashamed and humiliated.

For the past couple of days all of Joshua's friends had seen unheard of courage from Josh. He was the hero who could stand up to anyone. Now, Timmy, Robby, and Nick watched as their hero broke down and cried.

Levi was euphoric as he saw tears flow from Josh's eyes. It was just what he had wanted. He had finally broken the toughest of them.

Joshua looked to Cody one last time.

"Cody," he called desperately. His voice cracked, and tears covered his face.

Cody didn't look back. He remained silent.

Joshua turned towards the woods and ran as fast as he could. All he wanted to do was get away from everyone as fast as he could.

"Run away, faggot!" Levi shouted. "No one wants you here anymore!"

Cody thought he was going to throw up. His stomach muscles tensed so tightly he felt them strangling his lungs, forcing him to gasp for air. He desperately held back the tears from his face, as Levi's gang took turns giving him congratulatory pats on the back for the part he had played.

"You're pretty cool, Cody," Ken Fenton said.

The Scouts all followed Levi as he headed back to camp, bragging about his great victory all the way. Robby, Timmy, and Nick said nothing. They were still processing what they had witnessed. Joshua was the last person in the world they thought would be gay. They wanted an explanation.

CHAPTER EIGHT

*****

Cody wanted to go back and find Joshua, but he couldn't. Levi's gang walked with him all the way back to main camp. They took turns asking questions about Cody. He was their newest hero. It seemed that Robby was now also off limits as a target for bullying. He was Cody's friend, and that made Robby part of the gang by default.

"Hey, sorry I've been giving you such a hard time this week," Levi said to a dazed Robby. "We were just having fun. We didn't mean anything by it. You took it all pretty well. You're a pretty tough kid, you know that, Robin?"

Robby didn't expect Levi to use his nickname like that. Josh had given him that name, and he didn't like Levi using it.

"Thanks," Robby said inaudibly. He didn't know what else to do. Of course, he didn't have to say anything. Levi was doing all the talking.

"God, this must be horrible news for you. I mean, finding out you were tenting with a fag." Levi got a disgusted look on his face. "I mean, what if he saw you naked?" Levi asked. "I couldn't handle that. But like I said, you're pretty tough."

"Thanks," Robby repeated again, feeling ill at ease and wishing Levi would just shut up. It still hadn't sunk into him yet that Joshua was gay. It didn't seem to matter to Robby. The incident he had witnessed changed nothing. He was more concerned with the fact that Cody had set Joshua up. All Robby knew was that his friend was out in the woods somewhere alone and hurt. Josh would have been the first person to defend Robby in a similar situation. He felt guilty that he didn't have the courage to do likewise.

"Don't worry," Levi said to Robby. "I won't let any of this stick to you. If any of the kids accuse you of being gay, you just let me deal with them."

"Thanks," Robby muttered awkwardly one last time.

Levi put his arm around Robby, protecting him like a younger brother. Robby looked very uncomfortable but could do nothing. "Come on guys," Levi said, "let's find Pastor Bob before supper starts. We've got news for him."

*****

Pastor Bob walked towards the Trading Post where several other Scoutmasters were congregating. Many of them liked to gather informally right before dinner to discuss mutual problems or simply to pass the time. Pastor Bob missed most of these informal sessions, because he could never seem to find the group. This was a hint that he never seemed to get.

One of the Scoutmasters cringed when he saw Pastor Bob approaching them. The other Scoutmasters knew what that flinching meant. Only one person could provoke it. Pastor Bob had been coming to camp for some time, and he had quite a reputation. His abrasive nature towards his Scouts struck a few of the other Scoutmasters as excessively harsh. Since Pastor Bob was a man of God, however, no one ever thought to question him.

"Good afternoon," Pastor Bob greeted the others, as he approached.

"Likewise," one of them offered enthusiastically, if not genuinely. The artificiality in his tone was apparent to all except Pastor Bob.

"Well, I got to go and see what's up with my Scouts," one Scoutmaster quickly said, before anxiously getting up and slipping away.

The others wished they had done so first. Now they had to stay. It would be too obvious if anyone else got up and left. A few of them desperately hoped that Pastor Bob would go into the Trading Post and buy something before sitting down with them. Then they could sneak away less awkwardly. But Pastor Bob took the spot of the Scoutmaster who had just left, dashing their hopes.

"Greetings, Scouts," Pastor Bob said to two young boys who were catching a snack before dinner.

"Whatever," one of them responded, as he got up and walked away. His friend quickly joined him. Scouts didn't always show as much tact as adults did. That was one vice that all the Scoutmasters sitting at the Trading Post currently wish they had mastered.

Pastor Bob noted the silence that had taken over the conversation since his arrival. He didn't take it personally. He always assumed that people were simply naturally uncomfortable around him since he was a Pastor. He knew that it was up to him to kindle the conversation.

"So, Jack, I saw one of your boys playing Volleyball this morning," Pastor Bob said.

"Yeah, my troop reserved the court this morning for a game. They played against Trenton's troop," he said, hoping that Pastor Bob would talk to someone else now.

"Well, I was referring to one of your boys in particular, not the troop." Pastor Bob figured everyone knew who he meant, but no one reacted to his statement.

"I'm referring to that little kid, Frank or something. Whatever his name is, he obviously doesn't belong on that team." Pastor Bob believed he was just giving friendly advise and had no idea how obnoxious he sounded.

The Scoutmaster was angered by Pastor Bob's uninvited and uninformed critique, as most people would have been. He was especially mad, however, because Frank was his son. But the Scoutmaster took a deep breath and responded kindly. "Well, little Frank is rather new to Volleyball. He is just a little short for his age, that's all. He needs a little coaching, more practice, and some encouragement," the Scoutmaster defended.

He believed that would be enough to quiet Pastor Bob, but the other Scoutmasters had been around long enough to know better. They had never known Pastor Bob to back down on any argument, even when he knew he was wrong.

"The guy is a major wuss!" Pastor Bob finally teased, thinking he had just told a clever joke. No one laughed.

The Scoutmaster fumed inside but said nothing. He couldn't believe the nerve that Pastor Bob displayed. How dare he sit there and pick on a kid he didn't even know, the Scoutmaster felt.

"We can't all be Football players," another Scoutmaster jumped in, attempting to defend the first one.

Pastor Bob barely waited for him to finish his response before his retort. "A Scout is physically strong!" Pastor Bob shouted, quoting from the Scout Promise. "If your Scout can't cut it, then maybe he can join the Girl Scouts." Again, Pastor Bob thought he just scored another joke. Again, no one laughed.

The first Scoutmaster had finally had enough. He wasn't going to let this alleged man of God just sit there and pick on his son. But as the anger boiled up within him, it clouded out all of the wonderful insults he had just thought up.

For a moment, he almost said, "Fuck you." But he stopped himself. As he reassessed his response, the angry Scoutmaster saw a group of Scouts running towards them with tremendous speed. His anger turned to concern as he saw the anxiety in their eyes.

"Pastor Bob!" Levi yelled, as he got into hearing distance. He was nearly out of breath, but his words rolled out of his mouth effortlessly, riding on his excitement.

"Well, just who I wanted to see," Pastor Bob said to Levi. "We were just talking about that little wuss kid, Frank. You know who I mean, don't you?" Pastor Bob knew that Levi of all people would back him up.

Levi ignored him. He had his own concerns right now and didn't want to be distracted. "Josh is a fag!" he blurted out, as though some criminal had been let loose in camp.

By now, Cody and the rest of Levi's mob had caught up with him. Cody remained perfectly silent. He had never felt such fear in his life. He saw his father gaze at him, and he felt faint.

"Is it true?" Pastor Bob asked Cody quietly.

"Yes," Cody replied obediently, betraying his friend once again.

Pastor Bob said nothing. He looked down at the ground and took a deep breath. He slowly stood up. Usually, Pastor Bob was quite predictable, but none of the Scoutmasters knew what he was going to do next. They couldn't even fathom what had just happened.

Pastor Bob got up awkwardly. He obviously felt humiliated. He quickly looked around at the other Scoutmasters and gazed at each one of them directly in the eyes. The Scoutmasters dared not engage him back. They simply looked down.

Levi's news was demoralizing to him, but Pastor Bob wanted it clearly understood that this news didn't reflect poorly on him in any way. Manhood was very important to Pastor Bob, and his stare was a subtle reminder that no one dare challenge it. Making his point, Pastor Bob turned around and walked away. He was embarrassed beyond comprehension, but it didn't show.

The angry Scoutmaster had quietly observed the entire incident. His anger had momentarily subsided by the shocking revelation, but Pastor Bob's macho bravado rekindled his anger. As Pastor Bob walked away, the Scoutmaster knew that such a perfect chance for payback would never prevent itself again. Against his better judgment, he finally let Pastor Bob have it.

"So, it looks like you've got a wuss problem in your troop as well," he said to Pastor Bob. Everyone laughed.

None of the Scoutmasters gave a damn about how Joshua felt at that moment. They didn't care about the harsh treatment that he was bound to get when Pastor Bob found him. All they cared about was that Joshua had given them a perfect opportunity to get even. Joshua was a pawn they all used to get back some face.

Pastor Bob kept walking. He didn't respond to the laughter. He couldn't. He made his move, and they had challenged it. All he could do now was walk away, humbled and defeated.

*****

Joshua didn't know how far he had run or for how long. He desperately gasped for air but didn't stop running. It didn't matter to him where he was going. As he ran, he pushed his body to its limits.

When he felt tired, he increased his speed; when cramps gripped his chest, he ignored them. The harder he pushed his body, the more he had to concentrate on moving it and the more willpower it took to compensate for the overwhelming instinct to stop. The harder Joshua pushed, the less room there was in his head to contemplate what had just happened. Total concentration went into continuing his physical exertion.

All the willpower in the world, however, would not allow Joshua to continue to exceed his body's natural limits. Eventually, it began to weaken. His quick sprint slowed to a crawl; his steady course was replaced by recurrent stumbles. Joshua tried to correct his performance, but ultimately his body gave in, and he smashed into the ground. A moment of elation filled his body as it enjoyed the sudden relaxation of tension. Then everything rushed back to him, and Joshua felt the full force of reality drag him desperately back down into an inescapable dark void of despair.

The scene of his betrayal played itself out continually in his mind, like a movie clip caught in a loop. He couldn't stop the thoughts no matter how hard he tried. His mind no longer needed to concentrate on his body, as that had crashed. Unchained from his conscious will, his mind hurled every image of betrayal at him all at once. His thoughts became daggers, and they ripped his soul to pieces. Joshua desperately wanted the pain to stop. But the images wouldn't cease. His mind kept delivering them to him unhindered, no matter how hard he pleaded. His own mind betrayed him just as much as Cody had.

Joshua gazed at the blue sky through the tree-tops. His breathing was still shallow, but it was beginning to return to normal. How long had he lain there? Minutes? Hours? Time stood still for him. He hadn't moved since he collapsed. He gazed upwards into infinity, desperately hoping to lose himself in the immensity of space.

Slowly, Joshua's conscious mind began to reassert itself and take control of the agonizing barrage of hurtful memories. His emotions had run unencumbered, but now it was time for intellect to reassert itself. He felt a bottomless gash in his soul, but his mind began to prod him forward, offering him ideas and plans of action. Joshua was finally ready to decide upon his next move.

He realized he needed help; he needed someone to whom he could talk. But who could he trust anymore? His own best friend had just betrayed him. Joshua first considered leaving camp and wandering into town. It would be a 30 minute hike at best. Then, Josh figured, he could call his parents and have them pick him up. But this was an unsound option. His parents would demand some sort of explanation and would discover what had happened. Joshua couldn't bare that ordeal.

Joshua then thought about going to the camp chaplain. Given his experiences with Pastor Bob, however, Joshua quickly dismissed that idea as well. He had already experienced enough Christian compassion for one life.

Finally, an unexpected name emerged from Josh's subconscious, presenting him with a realistic option. Joshua didn't know why he hadn't thought of this person before. His emotions had obviously clouded his judgment. As reason reasserted itself, he now realized that Jim Meeder was the obvious choice. The two had their differences, but that was irrelevant now. Jim was the only person who could understand what Joshua was going through, and Joshua knew he had to find him.

The pain didn't stop, but Josh now had a plan. Despite falling into a deep desperate pit of despair, a plan of any sorts appeared like a ladder. He had to climb it.

As Joshua stood up, a head rush clouded his vision, and he crashed back into the ground. He lay there for a moment before trying again, this time standing up a little more slowly. Then he looked around and attempted to figure out where he had ended up. Nothing seemed familiar. He had no idea where he was, but he could hear the rippling water from the nearby lake. Once at the lake, Joshua realized, he could find a trail back to main camp. Then all he would have to do is keep out of sight until he found Jim.

*****

Only a few counselors were in the staff lounge this late in the afternoon. Most of the camp staff had just finished teaching merit badges all day, and they were quickly grabbing showers before dinner. But a few of the staff had gravitated to the staff lounge to seize a quick game of ping-pong before dinner. Jim Meeder decided to use his break to catch up on a book he had been reading.

He walked into the lounge and acknowledged his fellow counselors.

"What's up?" Jim asked, greeting no one in particular.

A few were engaged in an intense game of ping-pong. They still managed a token nod to Jim.

Another staff member was making out with his girlfriend in the corner. Wednesday was visitor's night after all, a time when parents and friends of campers could visit and see how their son was doing. Only campers who lived nearby, however, typically had any guests. Camp staff were always allowed visitors on this night as well, although like the regular visitors, such company was not supposed to arrive until after dinner.

Jim sat down on an old worn out couch in the corner of the lounge. He propped his legs up on a coffee table next to the couch and opened his book. The two ping-pong players were louder than Jim expected, so he had a difficult time concentrating on his book.

Suddenly, one of the players, Christopher, smashed the ping-pong ball at top speed onto his opponents' side. His opponent barely saw it coming and didn't have time to react. The ball slammed into his side of the table and raced by him, ending the game.

Christopher bellowed with glee. "He shoots; he scores!" he proclaimed while imitating a football touchdown dance.

His opponent smiled and walked over to pick up the ball. By the time he got it, Christopher was already pestering Jim Meeder, apparently looking for ego-stroking.

"Did you see that awesome shot?" he asked, demolishing Jim's attempted concentration.

"What?" Jim said, looking up. "Oh, yeah, nice move."

"Thanks. Glad to see that someone recognizes world-class talent."

"Enough already," his opponent announced. "Any more of this and your head will explode."

Chris was only teasing, of course. His friend had actually beaten him many times, and Chris knew he could do it again.

But dramatic presentations following a close win was all part of the fun.

Jim's attention soon returned to his book. He was starting to get annoyed at Chris but tried to ignore him. Jim always aimed to make the best use of his time, and he found this difficult to do with people interrupting his schedule. He preferred everything to go according to plan, his plan especially. Deviations from this ideal, even as slight as an unscheduled conversation, often annoyed him.

Chris and his friend finally got the message and began their own conversation. They didn't take Jim's attitude personally. They just knew he was like that sometime, and it was best to let him be.

A loud desperate knock on the door interrupted Jim once again. The thumping startled the two ping-pong players as well. No one ever knocked on the staff lounge door. Camp staff typically just walked in.

Tim went to answer the door, while Jim prepared to shout at whoever had interrupted his concentration yet again. He didn't anticipate what happened next.

A frightened young boy poked his head in and looked around, ignoring Chris, who had just opened the door for him. Jim's determined cold stare melted as he noticed it was Joshua.

"I need to talk to you," Joshua pleaded. His tone was desperate.

For a moment Jim thought Joshua had changed his mind about revealing their little secret. Jim's palms began to sweat as he contemplated the consequences of such a revelation. Jim knew he would lose his job in a second and probably all his friends as well.

He immediately put these thoughts aside. Joshua's tone was not that of a blackmailer. Something else was deeply bothering him, Jim could see.

Jim put his book aside, got up, and walked over to the door. As he walked out, Joshua quickly followed.

"What's wrong, guys?" Chris asked, as the two left the staff lounge.

"Nothing," Jim said coldly, not even looking back.

Chris got the message. Jim didn't want to be bothered.

*****

Jim could tell that Joshua was really distressed as the two left the staff lounge. He recalled the first time he had seen Joshua a few days ago. Josh possessed immense self-confidence. It seemed like no problem was insurmountable for him. Yet there he stood appearing lonely and desperate, almost hopeless.

"What's wrong?" Jim asked concerned, showing no sign of the annoyance he had in the staff lounge.

"They found out," Joshua cried desperately. "They know I'm gay." Tears rushed from his eyes, blurring his vision. Joshua felt the full onslaught of emotions from his betrayal seeping back into his being. He tried to hold them at bay, but he couldn't. Instinctively he reached forward and wrapped his arms around Jim, desperate for consolation, desperate for an anchor.

Jim didn't know what to do. Awkwardly, he put one arm around Joshua in a partial embrace. He looked around cautiously to make sure no one was looking. Only then did it occur to him that Joshua just came out to him. It now made perfect sense to Jim, and he figured that Cody must be gay as well.

"Did they find out about Cody, also?" Jim asked, trying to size up the situation.

"No, Cody's not gay. It was all a set-up. They tricked me. They knew all along." Joshua could barely speak amid his crying and difficulty breathing.

Jim pushed Joshua away from him, but not too hard. Jim was caught off guard by Josh's news. It made him realize how precarious a situation he himself was in. There had been rumors about Jim and his boyfriend, but they remained unconfirmed. No one really seemed to believe them. Jim had increasingly grown careless with his boyfriend, and Josh made him realize he needed to be more careful.

Chris walked out of the staff lounge and saw Joshua crying and desperately grasping onto Jim. "Is everything okay, guys?" he asked, confused by the scene.

"Yeah, fine," Jim replied, searching for an explanation. "Josh is just having a problem with a bully. It's nothing he can't handle."

"Oh," Chris replied, not completely convinced. But he left it up to Jim to handle.

Paranoia gripped Jim. He knew he couldn't afford to be seen with Joshua right now. People might suspect something.

"Listen, I can't help you. You have to leave. You shouldn't even be back here," Jim pleaded.

"What do I do?" Josh cried out.

"I don't know. Everything will be fine." Jim pulled away from Joshua and ran back into the staff lounge, leaving Joshua behind. Joshua stood there alone, with tears pouring down his face. He had no one else to whom he could turn.

CHAPTER 9

Everyone sat quietly at the dinner table, except for Joshua. His place was empty. Cody worried intensely about him. He wanted desperately to tell him what really happened - that the kiss wasn't a test, and that he really loved him. But Cody couldn't bring himself to go looking for Joshua, not with his father present.

Cody didn't eat anything at dinner. He still felt nauseous from the whole encounter in the woods. He had betrayed his best friend, and the pain, he believed, would last forever.

The front door of the Dining Hall opened, and Joshua quietly walked in. Almost no one noticed. Hundreds of people were busily eating and enjoying their own private conversations. But to Josh, it seemed like the whole world was staring at him. In reality, only two people noticed his presence. Cody fixated on Joshua the moment he walked in. So did Cody's father.

Pastor Bob got up and went to intercept Joshua as he walked to his table. He stepped in Josh's way but didn't say a thing. He simply pointed to a table at the back of the room. Joshua knew right away what it meant. The table was set aside for punishment. Those kids who misbehaved in some way or another were sent to sit apart from their friends, usually just for one meal. Supposedly this would humble and or humiliate the isolated Scout into behaving properly. It was the equivalent of the dunce cap.

Joshua and his friends had joked to themselves as to how many times Levi would be sitting at the dunce table throughout the week. But it was Joshua who would get there first. Josh turned and walked toward his new table, and Pastor Bob sat back down. No one waitered Josh's table; it was empty. He would have to get his own food. He just sat there and put his head on the table. He started to cry again. He no longer cared if everyone was staring at him. Nothing mattered.

*****

Cody now hoped to catch Joshua after dinner, but Joshua had run off as soon as supper ended and everyone was dismissed. Besides, Pastor Bob kept a close eye on Cody. He didn't want his son anywhere near that queer. He realized now why his son had defended gays a few days ago. Joshua must have been trying to convert his son, Pastor Bob reasoned. But Pastor Bob would not let that happen. He wouldn't let Cody get anywhere near Joshua.

Timmy, Robby, and Nick also complicated things logistically. Cody couldn't talk to Joshua with them around. He finally decided that the best time to find Joshua would be that night at the Order of the Arrow ceremony. He just hoped that Joshua would be okay until then.

Joshua walked over to the rock by the lake where Levi had sat after he had been evicted from his gang. He sat down and peered into the lake. His face was still covered in tears, but he was no longer crying.

He didn't notice Levi come up behind him. "Full circle, I guess," Levi called out, as he approached Joshua. Joshua saw that it was Levi and said nothing.

"Listen, I didn't mean for this to happen. I want to apologize," Levi said to Joshua in a sincere tone. Josh listened.

"Truth is, you're a pretty cool guy. I can't forget that you were the only one nice to me when I was alone. Don't get me wrong," he added, "I would never admit this to my gang."

Levi extended his hand. "Friends?"

Joshua didn't know how to respond. His pain ran so deep that he would have done or believed anything to stop it. As Levi extended his hand, Joshua dared to trust for that single moment that everything was going to be okay. Joshua reached out his hand in response. Levi grabbed it and pulled to help Joshua up. But half way up, he let go, and Joshua slammed into the rock.

"Psyche!" Levi yelled, as he began to laugh. "I hope you didn't think for one moment that I'd let a fag into my gang." He began to walk away, turning around to finish him off. "Think again, Queer Boy. You're on your own."

Joshua said nothing. He didn't cry. He didn't get mad. He wasn't sure what he felt. It seemed as though everything had gone numb, his body, his mind, his emotions, all went numb. A cool breeze from the lake blew through his hair. Josh felt nothing.

*****

Soon after dinner, Pastor Bob's troop gathered back at their campsite. Pastor Bob wanted everyone at one place where he could keep an eye on them. The Order of the Arrow ceremony would be starting soon, and he didn't want to have to track down all of his Scouts to ensure their promptness for the ceremony. That would make him look bad. The only Scout who wasn't back at camp was Joshua. Pastor Bob didn't know where Joshua went after dinner, nor did he care. He didn't want Joshua "contaminating" the rest of his Scouts.

Levi went back to his tent with his gang to kill time before the ceremony. His last encounter with Joshua still delighted him. His spirits were high. He invited Cody and his friends to join him, but they all declined. The boys feigned exhaustion and claimed they needed a quick nap before the ceremony. Levi didn't understand why his new friends weren't in a more festive mood, considering their victory over Joshua, but he didn't press matters. He liked his new friends now that they were on his side, and he had no problem working around their little quirks.

The troop had about an hour to kill before the OA ceremony, and most of them didn't have a difficult time finding something to do. Levi's group retired to the privacy of their tent for their victory celebration. Other Scouts started up a fire and engaged in superficial banter. Pastor Bob called his assistant Scoutmaster to his tent in order to discuss Joshua with him. Timmy and Nick went back to their tent for their alleged nap. Cody and Robby did likewise.

Robby lay quietly on his sleeping bag as Cody entered the tent. This was the first time they had been alone together since Cody had betrayed Joshua. Robby closed his eyes, but Cody knew he was awake. Tension thickened the room. It was inconceivable to Robby how easily Cody had betrayed Joshua. Robby had gotten to know Cody rather well over the past couple of days, and along with Joshua, considered him his best friend. How could he have been so wrong about Cody? He said nothing to him. His rage silently boiled up.

Cody suffered the tension, not knowing what else to do. He couldn't explain what had really happened. No one could know the truth about his sexual orientation, especially his father. His fear of being discovered consumed him and eclipsed any hope that he could trust anyone with his secret.

"Hey, I got an idea," Cody said excitedly, trying to break the ice with Robby. "Let's do some more songs. I still think that photographic mind of yours has its limits." Cody knew his suggestion was lame even as he said it.

Robby turned on his side, facing away from Cody. He remained silent.

This was going to be more difficult than Cody thought, but he persisted. "Okay, do the words to 'MMMBop,' by Hanson."

"No!" Robby shouted. "I don't want to do your damn songs!" He added sarcastically, "Besides, don't you think that song is rather gay?"

That stung hard. Cody saw that he could cut Robby's disdain for him with a knife. It allayed any doubts he still had left that he could make things better again. But at some level, he was glad for it. Robby was a decent person, and any decent person, Cody believed, should hate him for what he had done. Cody understood Robby's hatred and even shared it. He hated himself right now more that anyone else could. But he still pressed on. He had to talk to someone. Any amount of chatter allowed him to bury his thoughts and avoid confronting his betrayal of Joshua.

"Okay, how about something by Pearl Jam?" Cody pleaded.

"Look, Cody, I'm tired!" Robby angrily responded. "Just leave me alone." Robby turned and lay on his stomach this

time. It was increasingly difficult to feign a conversation.
Cody knew it was hopeless.

The sound of his tent flap unzipping gave him a momentary
reprieve. But when Timmy and Nick walked in, Cody got
anxious. His stomach muscles tightened, and sweat appeared
on his forehead. He wanted desperately to avoid being alone
with his other friends. He knew they would want to discuss
what happened. Cody was less terrified of being alone with
Robby, because Robby was too mad to talk about it. But now
the dreaded conversation seemed inevitable.

"Hi guys," Nick said in soft and sullen voice, as the two
crawled into the tent. Cody grabbed for his shoes and explained
to them that he had to get to a meeting with his father. Though
convenient, such meetings were not entirely unbelievable.
Cody was a leader in the troop, and as such, he had to
constantly touch base with his father. Cody tried not to look
obvious as he frantically scampered out the tent door. Robby
waited for Cody to make his exit before turning around and
acknowledging the presence of his friends.

"Hi guys," Robby uttered quietly. He wasn't mad at them.
They were as innocent as he was. They didn't know that Cody
had been plotting with Levi all along. They were all equally
stunned by the revelation.

"We need to talk about this," Robby said confidently.

"We already did that a little," Timmy said. "We couldn't
believe it," he asserted. "It's the last thing in the world we
expected."

"Me too," Robby agreed, "I was so pissed at him."

"We were surprised," Nick continued, sounding confused,
"but we didn't get pissed. Why were you mad?"

"He betrayed him," Robby asserted. "Why else?"

"What are you talking about?" Nick asked.

"What are you talking about?" Robby returned.

"I'm talking about Joshua being gay," he said, thinking that was obvious.

The only thing obvious to Robby was that they had been having two entirely different conversations. Robby hadn't even thought yet about Joshua being gay. All his attention had been focused on his anger at Cody for betraying Joshua.

"I was talking about Cody setting up Joshua like that," Robby stated.

Nick and Timmy looked at each other confused.

"Hello," Robby said sarcastically. "You know, Joshua, our friend?"

"Oh, that," Nick finally responded reluctantly.

"Yes, that," Robby interrupted. "That is the only issue here!"

Nick felt ashamed for a moment. Robby had asserted himself so forcefully that for a moment Nick knew that Robby was right. But on the surface, he concentrated on Joshua being gay. That was what he thought most people would be concerned about, so that's what he thought about.

"Yeah," said Timmy, as he slapped Nick upside the head. "I told you that was the real issue."

"If that's the issue," Nick asked, still sounding confused, "then how are we any different from Cody?"

"Yeah," Timmy agreed. This whole conversation had been very difficult for him. He finally decided that agreeing with everyone was probably the best tactic.

"What do you mean?" Robby questioned, already knowing the answer.

"Why are we here and not with Joshua? We betrayed him too. We just stood there and let Levi have at him. We didn't stand up for him. How are we any different?"

Robby lay back on his sleeping bag. He turned and faced away from his friends.

"Well?" Nick pressed.

"We're not!" Robby screamed, facing his friends again. "We're not any different!" Robby broke into tears.

Timmy and Nick said nothing. Neither did Robby. The three sat there not knowing what to do or say.

"Still, it just seems a bit strange," Nick finally offered, breaking the silence. Nick had the least inhibitions about discussing taboo subjects. For him it was best simply to talk about things. He didn't always agree with what came out of his mouth, but he always said something, usually stuff he heard elsewhere. Parroting accepted wisdom was a good way to test it, he felt.

"Why is it so strange?" Timmy asked. "I mean, everyone knows gay people exist."

"Yeah, but who would have thought that Joshua was one of them?" He doesn't look anything like a gay person," Nick said.

"Obviously he does," Robby stated.

"Yeah," Timmy agreed, having nothing of his own to add.

"I guess now the question is, where do we stand on this? Are we with Joshua or Levi?" Robby asked. He looked to Nick first.

"Well?" he pressured.

"Of course we are with Joshua," Nick said. "I was just a little shocked, that's all."

"Timmy?" Robby pressed next.

"I'm with Joshua," Timmy agreed. "And with you," he added.

"So, what do we do now?" Nick prodded, looking for direction. Evidently Robby was their new leader.

Robby lay back again on his sleeping bag and gazed up at the tent ceiling. "I don't know what we do now," he said. "I just don't know."

"Yeah," Nick agreed. "The Scout Handbook really doesn't address this."

Tim and Robby almost laughed in response.

*****

Joshua sauntered back to camp on an isolated path. As he arrived, it was about 8:00 p.m., and all his troop-mates were lining up getting ready to leave for the Order of the Arrow ceremony. Joshua had forgotten all about it. He had been excited about the ceremony ever since Cody first told him it honored Native American traditions, but now he just didn't care.

Pastor Bob spotted Joshua as he walked back into camp. He chided him for being late and ordered him to the back of the line. Everyone looked at Josh but tried not to act like it. By now everyone knew about him. Levi and Pastor Bob had made sure of that.

Joshua obediently took his place at the back of the line. He hadn't met any of these Scouts yet. They were younger than him, probably Robby's age, he deduced. They all got quiet as he approached and took his place. As the troop leader, Cody was at the front of the line. Nick, Timmy, and Robby were right behind him. Joshua noticed Robby look back at him for a second, but Robby quickly turned his head forward, as Pastor Bob prompted him to.

After waiting in line for about five minutes, two Scouts dressed like Indian guides arrived to escort them to the ceremony. The guides were counselors dressed only in loin cloths. They had black and red Indian paint on their faces and carried ceremonial spears decked out in feathers. The guides informed everyone that they would be led to the ceremonial area to witness a sacred ceremony. They asserted that everyone must remain absolutely silent until the end of the ceremony. This effectively created a reverent mood. After finishing their instructions, the guides led the troop out of the campsite and over to the ceremonial area.

The Scouts could hear Indian drumming as they approached the ceremony. The ceremony was held in a area in the forest that naturally indented into the ground like a giant bowl. It was surrounded by hills about twenty feet high. Logs had been placed into the hill for seats. Torches lit the trail that led directly into the ceremonial area. Hundreds of Scouts from all over camp were arriving and being seated by the Indian guides. Parents who had arrived for visitor's night had already been seated. It was quite a spectacle. No one was talking.

At the bottom of the ceremonial bowl, there was a huge sand painting of a giant eagle. Two huge stacks of carefully arranged firewood towered at about five feet each, dominating the central stage. It must have taken hours to create.

Joshua's troop was the last to arrive, and the ceremony began soon after they were seated.

An Indian guide walked out and explained the legend that inspired the Order of the Arrow. He told of a tribe of Delaware Indians called the Lene Lenape, who were endangered by approaching enemies. The chief of the Lene Lenape called for volunteers from the tribe to go and warn neighboring Indians about these enemies, but no one volunteered. The tribe members felt that they should not risk their own lives to help strangers. Finally two warriors came forward. The two stated that all Indians were brothers, included their neighboring tribes, and they volunteered to go and warn them. The chief was so impressed by their courage and sense of brotherhood that he created the Order of the Arrow to honor their bravery. Each year, the chief explained, those Scouts who exemplified such ideals would be inducted. They had to be "unselfish in the service and devotion to the welfare of others," the guide explained.

Cody had told Joshua earlier that their troop had voted its members in before Joshua arrived. No one would know who from their troop had been inducted until that night. First year Scouts were the only ones excluded from the Order.

Those who were inducted would spend the night and the following day going through an initiation. They would be required to spend the night alone in the woods and perform service projects for the camp the next day. They would not be allowed to talk and would be given very little food. Joshua immediately recognized that the ceremony partly simulated a Native American "Vision Quest" ritual.

A shaman figure walked into the ceremonial area and said a prayer to recognize the powers of the four sacred directions. This was followed by an Eagle dance and Buffalo dance in which an Indian imitated the life cycle of these creatures. The life cycle of the animal was tied to the lives of the people, demonstrating an intimate connection between the two.

Eventually, the narration and the Indian dancing came to an end. The area was taken over by the Great Chief who stood quietly at the center of the circle, while two Indian guides representing the original two selfless Indians walked sternly through the audience to the beat of drums. Whenever the drum beat stopped, the guides ran and picked a single Scout from the various troops and brought him before the chief. The chief then tapped the candidate gently three times on the shoulder and sat him down in front of the audience.

The Scouts tensed up every time the Indian guides approached. When the drums stopped beating, anyone could be grabbed and brought up before the Chief. Only the first year Scouts knew that they were not eligible and thus could afford a degree of security.

Joshua had a difficult time concentrating on the ceremony. His mind was on the events that had destroyed his life over the past couple of hours. Even as he sat there, occasionally eyeing Cody, he could not believe what had happened. He had felt closer to Cody than to anyone in his entire life. Never before had he opened himself up so much to anyone; never before had he become so vulnerable. How could he have been so mistaken about Cody?

Cody was also having a difficult time concentrating on the ceremony. His thoughts raced through the days events. Fear of his father so overwhelmed him that he betrayed his best friend to avoid it. But the guilt he now felt seemed equally strong. He had to confront Cody, his father be damned. Cody decided he would talk to Joshua immediately after the ceremony, no matter who was around. He would explain to him how he really felt. He couldn't let Josh go on believing that he was one of Levi's friends.

Cody got so preoccupied with his intended confrontation with Joshua that he forgot about the Indian ceremony before him. Cody was a third year Scout and very popular with the troop. He was a prime candidate for the Order. The younger Scouts especially respected him and no doubt had voted for him. That thought was not on his mind.

The drum beat stopped, and one of the two Indian guides instantly grabbed Cody and escorted him over to the Chief. Cody barely knew what had happened. He had just been sitting there deep in thought. Now the Indian chief gazed deep into Cody's eyes. His face was painted in white and black, and he wore a long feathered headdress.

"Look into my eyes and do not flinch," he said, before proceeding to tap Cody on the shoulders three times. Another Indian guide then seated Cody with the other candidates. That was it. He had been inducted. "What do I do now?" he thought to himself, unable to concentrate on the great honor just bestowed on him. Following this ceremony, Cody would be led to a special ritual held only for the candidates. There they would further learn of the legends associated with the Order. He would be separated from Joshua and the rest of his troop until the next night when the initiation was over. There was always the chance that he would run into Joshua while doing service projects around camp throughout the day, but he would not be allowed to talk again until the initiation was complete. Silence was enforced. Cody felt terrible realizing that Joshua would spend the next twenty-four hours believing he had been betrayed.

Cody snapped back to attention as he saw one of the Indian guides pull Levi from the crowd and bring him before the chief. Cody couldn't believe it. Evidently enough people felt Levi's complete denigration of other human beings was admirable enough to induct him into Scouting's highest honor. It was amazing to Cody that someone like Levi could garnish a single vote, let alone enough to get elected into the Order of the Arrow. Cody suspected his father may have had something to do with this.

Joshua himself was not surprised by anything anymore. He sat there with contempt as he watched the two people, who conspired to humiliate him, get recognized for their unselfish concern for others. To Joshua, this was the greatest blasphemy and perversion of Native American beliefs that could possibly be committed. For the first time since he had been betrayed, he felt no real pain. That emotion was temporarily shoved aside. As he watched Levi being tapped on the shoulders and led over to Cody, he could feel nothing but contempt.

*****

The ceremony ended about 10:00 p.m. The Scouts were cleared out of the area and went back to their campsites to get ready for bed. The OA candidates waited behind for their trial to begin. Two counselors dressed as Indians instructed the candidates to head back to their campsites, pick up their sleeping bags, and return within half an hour. "No talking," they were warned. Cody was relieved to hear this, as he realized he could now talk to Joshua after all. Of course, he would have to violate his oath not to talk, but that was the last thing on his mind.

Cody tried to avoid Levi as he walked back to camp, but Levi caught up with him. They were the only two inductees from their troop, and they walked quietly back together. Cody was surprised that Levi remained silent. He was sure that Levi would violate the oath. But Levi seemed to be taking this all very seriously, almost as though he was proud of his initiation.

Equally surprising, Levi hadn't teased Cody at all since that afternoon. He accepted Cody as a member of his gang. Levi knew that no one else in his band would have gone to the lengths that Cody had in order to reveal a fag in the troop. Levi felt indebted to Cody for getting even with Joshua for him. Cody was one brave kid in Levi's eyes.

Levi and Cody entered their campsite. Their troop-mates were already in their tents and settling down for the night. A few strays were still brushing their teeth. Cody could hear soft conversations going on as he walked past each tent on his way towards his own. Mostly, everyone was talking about the ceremony they had just seen. It was a rather mesmerizing presentation, especially for the newest campers.

As Cody approached his tent, he thought about Robby. Could he somehow get Robby to let them be alone for a few minutes? But it quickly occurred to Cody that his father probably moved Robby out of the tent. Pastor Bob wasn't allowing anyone even to talk with Joshua, let alone to sleep in the same tent with him.

Cody mentally rehearsed what he was going to say to Joshua. But he didn't know how he could ever face him again. How would Joshua react? Finally, he decided that even if Joshua hated him forever, he still had to tell him what really happened, and that their kiss was real. He could no longer bare the thought that Joshua felt betrayed and humiliated by him.

Cody arrived at his tent. As he reached for the zipper, his stomach muscles tensed and adrenaline shot through his body. He felt nauseous again, but he pushed on. He was determined to talk to Josh. He pulled the flap open and crawled in. The tent was dark.

"Joshua," Cody whispered quietly, grabbing for his flashlight. But there was no response. Cody knew this wasn't going to be easy, and he knew that Joshua was hurt and probably angry. But he hadn't expected the silent treatment. He turned on his light and pointed it towards Joshua's side of the tent. Josh's sleeping bag sat in the corner crumpled up just as it had been that morning. Joshua hadn't been back to the tent. Various scenarios ran through Cody's mind, none of them good. The worst case scenario, suicide, was all he could think about. Cody fled his tent frantically, and ran to his father's tent as fast as he could.

"Dad, Joshua is gone!" he yelled, not fearing the consequences.

"Damn it, Cody! You are supposed to be getting back to the ceremony, and you are not to talk!" Pastor Bob shouted angrily.

"Dad, he's gone!" Cody cried out, ignoring his father's concerns.

Pastor Bob knew immediately that Cody was talking about Joshua. "He was brushing a minute ago. He'll be back in a minute! Now get back immediately!" his father commanded.

"Now!" he screamed furiously at his confused son.

For a second, Cody thought that his father might strike him. But Cody was still relieved. Joshua was all right after all. But Cody couldn't talk to Joshua now. His father eyed him as he left the campsite. Cody would have to wait until another time.

Pastor Bob hadn't really seen Joshua. He had no idea where Joshua was at that moment. Nor did he care. Pastor Bob was more concerned with how the other Scoutmasters would perceive him now that they knew he had a homosexual in the troop.

As Cody walked quietly down the trail back to the ceremonial area, he heard footsteps walking in the same direction several hundred feet ahead of him. He reasoned that it was Levi, but it wasn't. Joshua had left the campsite not knowing that Cody was right behind him anymore than Cody knew that Joshua was ahead of him. They walked the trail in the dark, both silent, both alone. But they had two different destinations in mind. Cody was heading for his initiation. Joshua headed someplace further out; he was heading to Tommy's Point.

*****

Joshua could bare no more. His troop was embarrassed to be around him, Pastor Bob saw him as an abomination, and his best friend deceived him for a laugh. And things were only going to get worse. Pastor Bob would soon inform his parents what had happened. He would have no friends at school, and his parents would make life a living hell for him at home. They might even try to "cure" him!

He was alone now, and it was pitch dark as he walked down the Tommy Point Trail. Joshua didn't care anymore about the monster. Let it take him, if it existed. It could only end his misery.

He finally reached Tommy's Point. Clouds covered the night sky, and an eerie silence pervaded the surroundings. The lake was calm.

Joshua walked to the edge of the cliff and looked down at the rocks below. He was surprised at how much the scene resembled the one in his dreams, especially since he had never been there before in real life.

Joshua could almost see the image from his dreams of Tommy's cold, dead body lying naked on the rocks below. His pain momentarily transformed into anger as he recalled the Demon that had so coldheartedly and viciously pushed Tommy off the cliff.

"Coward!" Joshua shouted out loud, wanting the monster to hear him. "Why don't you come for me!"

His voice echoed down the lake. Joshua waited a few seconds, half expecting a response. "What's the matter?" he shouted. "Damn you, take me!"

There was no response. No monster came out of the woods to kill Joshua. Just that eerie silence.

Joshua contemplated for a moment ending everything himself. It would be easier to jump than to continue experiencing so much pain. Who would even care?

He laid down on the cliff's edge and stared up at the clouds. He thought more about Cody and when he had "come out" to him. Josh realized now that Cody's coming out must have been part of the plan. He began to cry once again.

Joshua thought about praying to the spirits for a vision, something that would help him make sense of everything that had happened. But, he couldn't. Right now he didn't believe in the spirits.

It felt like hours had gone by, but it could have been minutes. Joshua lost all sense of time. He could no longer distinguish between reality and dream. He felt a cool breeze from the lake and sensed a storm was approaching. That was his last thought before the dream world claimed him. Now he would have to deal with the Demon.

*****

Jumbled images vied for dominance in Joshua's mind, as his dream displayed scenes seemingly for review. Tommy Drapos cowered before the bullies in his troop, crying frantically for them to stop. Tommy ran through the woods desperately attempting to escape the dark Creature chasing him. Tommy's mangled body lay cold and dead as the rain drops pelted it from the storm.

These scenes played themselves over and over again while Joshua's subconscious desperately tried to make sense of them. Joshua consciously knew that the Demon didn't exist. He had just confronted that fear, and the Creature didn't show. But something was closing in on Tommy, something pushed him off the edge of that cliff.

Tommy ran faster and faster as the Demon appeared. But Joshua could see no monster. All he heard was the laughter from the kids. The laughter itself seemed to take on form and stalked Tommy, sinisterly prodding him forward.

Lightening flashed madly, and the thunder was deafening.

Tommy stopped once again before the cliff. Joshua looked carefully, and this time he saw the Demon thing approaching the terrified Tommy Drapos from behind. It held out a bloodied stick and laughed furiously. It was a childish sounding laugh, perfectly imitating the voices of his troop-mates who had raped Tommy with the stick.

The dark figure hurled the stick down and screamed "faggot!" before bursting forward in a surge of rage at Tommy, knocking him off the cliff. Once again, Joshua witnessed Tommy's body slam into the rocks below.

CHAPTER NINE

"No!" Joshua screamed, enraged by the actions of the Demon.

It turned towards Joshua. But instead of fear, Josh only felt confused. Something kept reminding him that the Creature was an illusion. But there it stood staring at him. Joshua tried to believe that it wasn't real, as it approached. The Demon's face remained blurred as it got closer to Joshua. Joshua stood his ground. He didn't run this time. He had no reason to. It could not hurt him anymore. Nothing could, Joshua realized.

Suddenly, a bright light appeared from above. The rain stopped, and a break in the clouds exposed a radiant full moon. As the light struck the Devil, it came into focus for the first time. Joshua gazed directly at Levi where the dark form had been standing. Then another flash of lightning temporarily blinded him. He opened his eyes, and now Pastor Bob stood before him as the face of the monster. Another flash, as the Creature got even closer, revealed Cody. And then, the images melted into each other and became one.

"Fucking queer!" the three faces of the Monster said simultaneously, but in different voices resonating as one. The Demon reached forward with its colossal hands and grabbed for Joshua's throat. It lifted Joshua up by the neck with no trouble and squeezed. Joshua felt the air rush out from his lungs as he gasped for air. He instantly awoke, as the sun began to rise above the eastern part of the lake.

Joshua sat up and took a second to get his bearings. He was not sweating this time. He remembered his dream and knew for the first time what it all meant. He had gotten a vision after all. He had been right. The Demon did not exist. But something did in fact shove Tommy off that cliff. It was Tommy's own fellow Scouts. The Demon was human.

CHAPTER 10

Joshua heard voices as he walked past the Order of the Arrow ceremonial grounds on his way back to camp. It was only about 6:00 a.m., and it surprised Joshua that campers were up so early. Usually he was the only one who got up that early.

Then he remembered the Order of the Arrow ceremony from the night before. It seemed like so long ago. The voices he heard were from counselors overseeing various work projects. These taskmasters woke up all the candidates early to begin their long day of work projects.

Joshua peeped into the ceremonial area through the trees. He saw Cody yank at some dead branches and drag them over to the fire, still smoldering from the previous night's ceremony. They were restocking the area with firewood for next weeks' ceremony, when a new batch of Scouts would be inducted.

Cody looked terrible. His hair stood up, his clothes were wrinkled, and his eyes betrayed a lack of sleep. But he also looked dreadful beyond simply the physical sense.

Joshua didn't know exactly what Cody was feeling, but he seemed depressed. Joshua was overcome by sympathy. For an instant, he saw only the boy he had fallen in love with, not the boy who betrayed him. For a moment it was as though the events of the previous day had never occurred. But they had, and Josh snapped back to the present.

CHAPTER TEN

Cody looked up into the forest and caught Josh's stare. The two gazed at each other, seemingly mesmerized. Neither could do or say anything.

Tears began to collect in Joshua's eyes as he remembered his feelings towards Cody. His first instinct was to turn and run. But he didn't. He continued to peer at Cody, and the tears kept falling.

Cody noticed the tears and couldn't bare what he had done. He felt the pain he had inflicted on his friend. Cody never thought of himself as an evil person. He had always been kind to other people. He befriended new kids and never picked on anyone. He used to think that was all that mattered. But these past couple of days taught him that being a good person meant something more. It meant courage. It wasn't the hateful bigotry of Levi or Pastor Bob that destroyed Joshua, Cody realized, it was Cody's compliance with it.

Finally, Joshua turned and ran. Cody stood there and watched his friend disappear into the woods.

"Get to work," one of the taskmasters called to Cody, noticing that he had slacked off. Cody ignored him and just kept staring into the woods. He knew that he should be with Joshua right now, no matter the consequences. That was what a true friend would do.

"Hey!" the taskmaster called again. "I said get to work."

Cody snapped to awareness as he realized that the taskmaster was addressing him. He turned back to the branches and continued to pull at them until they were loosened from the shrubbery in which they were lodged. He dragged them over to the fire and broke them up before adding them to the wood pile. A tear gently fell from his eye and ran down his face. The taskmaster noticed it and figured he got a speck of dust in his eye. Soon there was another tear and then another.

"Are you okay?" the taskmaster asked, starting to get concerned.

Cody looked him in the eyes. He was crying uncontrollably.

"No," he whimpered, unable to contain the tears. The taskmaster stood there confounded, as Cody took off as fast as he could towards the trail where he had just seen his friend. Damn the consequences, Cody thought to himself. All that mattered was finding Joshua.

*****

Levi sat at the Trading Post chugging down a soda. He was sweating profusely. Levi, too, had been awakened early to begin work projects. But one of the taskmasters had sent him to the tool shed to bring back some equipment.

Levi sat there with the shovels and two saws that he had been told to bring back. He saw no harm in grabbing a soda on his way back. Very few people were up yet, and no one would notice, he reasoned.

Levi figured that it must be getting close to 7:00 a.m., as crowds were starting to gather. Mostly, people were heading down to the showers located near the Trading Post.

Also, the Aquatics area was holding an "early bird" swim that morning, bringing more people into main camp than normal. Levi wanted to finish his soda and get back to the other inductees before anyone noticed him violating his initiation.

Levi's gang piled into main camp. They were in their bathing suits and had towels around their necks. Though they had been thrown out of the lakefront, they figured that since

Levi wasn't around, the lifeguards wouldn't remember their infraction.

"Shit," Levi said quietly to himself. Maybe his friends wouldn't notice him, he hoped. Maybe they would just walk on by.

"Hey Levi!" Ken Fenton yelled.

"Look guys, its Levi!" The group ran over to greet their fearless leader.

"Hey, congratulations man," one of the gang said.

"Yeah," another boy jumped in. "We know you can't talk or anything, but hey, good luck."

Levi was surprised. He figured they would rag on him or something. But evidently they thought the whole Order of the Arrow thing was pretty cool. It was hard not to after the impressive ceremony the night before. It had a certain mystique to it that captivated everyone who watched it.

One kid noticed the soda in Levi's hands. "It looks like they're treating you pretty well," he said.

Levi just smiled.

"Well, we'll let you get back to work. We see you have a lot to do," Ken Fenton observed, noticing the tools next to Levi.

"Yeah," another boy said. "See ya, Levi. Good luck."

Joshua entered main camp as he left the trail from the ceremonial area. The gang noticed him immediately. Ken even waved to him, before remembering that they were enemies.

Joshua saw the gang as well, but he ignored them. He just kept walking towards the campsite trail, seemingly oblivious to the fact that everyone was staring at him. Even Scouts from other troops were staring at him now. Stories traveled fast at camp.

Levi and his band could not resist the opportunity to humiliate Joshua one more time. They had already hurt him as much as possible, but that was yesterday. They were especially tempted by the fact that Joshua was ignoring them.

"Looking for your boyfriend, faggot!" Levi yelled instinctively. After saying it, Levi remembered that he wasn't supposed to talk. But his friends didn't even notice. They were having too much fun. Their leader was at it again. The gang figured that Levi's simple tease was probably the end of it.

But it wasn't the end of it. Josh halted as he heard Levi's comment. An image of Tommy Drapos' mangled body entered Joshua's head. The poor kid just lay there dead, murdered, Joshua realized, by bastards like Levi. Joshua turned and faced Levi from a distance. A pent up anger raged within him. He determined that he was not going to be the next Tommy Drapos.

Joshua peered into Levi's eyes intently and began to walk towards him. Most of Levi's gang had already turned away from Joshua, figuring he had already disappeared into the woods.

By the time Levi turned his attention back to Joshua, it was too late. Joshua came up from behind him. He leaped over the log that Levi was sitting on and grabbed Levi's hair as he flew over him. Momentum did the rest. Levi's head and body flew forward, as Josh pulled him from the log. Levi bumped his head on the handle of his shovel as he smashed into the ground.

"You fucking queer!" Levi shouted at the top of his lungs.

This was the wrong thing to say. Joshua could not think about anything except tearing Levi to pieces. Joshua stepped forward to attack. Levi saw him coming and swung his fists. Joshua grabbed Levi by the wrist and used his thrust against him. He twisted Levi's wrists and yanked him forward. Before

Levi knew it, Joshua had Levi's arm behind his back. Joshua shoved his arm upward, and Levi screamed in pain.

"Damn it, you fucking queer!" Levi yelled again, this time his voice cracking from the pain. Tears rushed down his face.

Joshua grabbed a handful of Levi's hair with his free hand and pulled Levi's head back. "I suggest you stop saying that," Joshua yelled furiously. His voice trembled with anger.

"Fuck you!" Levi yelled.

But Joshua was determined to continue until Levi yielded. He was not going to accept anything less than total defeat. Joshua pulled Levi by the hair and slammed him face first into the bark of a nearby tree. Again, Levi screamed in pain. Blood rushed down his face. Josh slammed Levi's face again into the bark of the tree. He then pushed Levi's face upward, scraping his face against the coarse bark. As the skin on Levi's face chafed against the bark, his skin broke and blood poured from his face.

Levi screamed again. Joshua continued to hold him in place. He was in complete control. Joshua had immediate access to numerous pressure points. If Levi tried to escape, Joshua would inflict more pain. Levi realized that he was helpless and began to cry.

"You fucking bastard!" Joshua screamed. "Beaten by a queer. How does it feel?" he shouted. The rage engulfed him and Joshua felt powerful.

"Answer me!" Joshua screamed, before Levi had a chance to say anything.

"No," Levi whimpered.

"Let's hear it! Apologize!"

"I'm sorry," Levi said admitting defeat, no longer able to bare the pain. But then Levi saw something and realized he had not been defeated just yet. He could try one more thing. In the distance, Levi saw his new friend, Cody, heading right towards them.

Cody entered camp, looking for Joshua, and immediately saw him and Levi fighting. He ran towards them. Levi realized that only Cody could beat Joshua now. Just like he had before.

"Cody! I think your little friend misses you," Levi yelled out loud. Levi was laughing again. He knew seeing Cody had to hurt Joshua more than anything he could do. Betrayal was the ultimate pain.

Joshua turned his head and saw Cody standing there. He loosened his grip. Levi escaped and turned toward Joshua with a smile.

"Still got a soft spot in your heart for your old boyfriend, Indian Boy? I mean Queer Boy." Levi's friends laughed.

"Tell him, Cody. Tell Joshua what we think of fags."

Cody had expected to find Joshua alone, where he could tell him what had really happened. But instead he found himself in the same situation as before. If he defended Joshua, everyone would know that he was gay.

"Tell him," Levi yelled. "Tell the faggot he has no friends here!"

Joshua couldn't stand it anymore. He felt like he was going to cry. He didn't want to be humiliated again, not like this. He turned and began to walk away.

"Red Feather," he heard Cody call. Joshua stopped and turned around to face Cody.

"It's not true," Cody said shaking. "The kiss was real," he confessed right there in front of everyone. His voice began to crack and his hands were shaking. "I was scared they would find out that I'm gay. I didn't want to hurt you, but I was so scared. I'm so sorry." Tears collected in his eyes.

Levi stood there dumbfounded.

"What did you say?" Levi asked, unable to believe what he just heard. "What did you say!?" he repeated loudly this time.

Cody rubbed his eyes clean and stepped up next to Levi. He peered directly into his eyes and then shouted at the top of his voice. "I said I'm gay!" Cody felt a tremendous sense of relief. He noticed that several Scouts had stopped and were staring at him.

Cody looked around. "Did anyone not hear me?" he asked sarcastically. He then faced Levi again. "So, now what do you got?" Cody challenged.

Joshua walked over to Cody and put his arm on Cody's shoulder. They embraced. Joshua was stunned by everything that had happened. The past twenty-four hours seemed like a bad dream, which had just ended. Cody had not betrayed him after all. Cody grabbed Joshua by the arm and the two ran off together towards their campsite trail. Everyone looked at them. They didn't care.

"You better run," Levi yelled as the two boys disappeared into the forest. "You better believe I'm telling your father!"

*****

Joshua and Cody reached the entrance to the trail as they headed back to their campsite. Cody was still trembling from the incident with Levi. They saw Robby up ahead on the trail coming towards them. Timmy and Nick trailed close behind.

The three boys had seen the entire incident. Cody and Joshua stopped in front of them and said nothing.

"We've been looking for you," Robby said to Cody in a tough tone.

Joshua stepped forward threateningly, prepared to defend Cody. "You gotta problem?" he asked.

"Damn right," Nick responded. Robby finished for Nick. "We have some friends who are in trouble, and we don't know how to help them. But we want them to know that they are not alone."

Joshua was especially surprised by this. He had expected no help from his former friends. He expected the sort of reactions given by Levi and Pastor Bob. But acceptance?

Joshua didn't know what to say. He knew that he and Cody needed help but had no idea what could be done at this point. "Your father is going to kill us," Joshua said candidly to Cody. "We do need their help."

"Yeah," Robby said. "He totally hates you, Red Feather. Robby paused for a second as if contemplating his next words. Then he declared, "Pastor Bob is a real fucker." Nick put his arm around Robby's mouth. "You're getting too good at those words, Robin."

Timmy chimed in. "Robin is right, though. There is no reasoning with your father," he explained to Cody.

"Maybe that's the problem," Cody said. Joshua and Robby looked at each other perplexed. They saw that look in Cody's eyes and immediately recognized it. It was the same look he had when he so skillfully manipulated his father after Jim Meeder had tossed Josh out of Citizenship merit badge.

"What do you mean?" Robby mumbled. Nick's hand still covered his mouth.

CHAPTER TEN

"Maybe it's time we be as irrational as he is," Cody offered. The group was intrigued.

They walked together back to main camp. The friends knew Cody had a plan, but he wouldn't tell them what. "Just follow my lead," he kept saying. He appeared confident and undeterred. But really, he was terrified.

*****

The Camp Director, Aaron Henderson, walked around main camp, apparently looking for something. Most of the Scouts could tell something was up. No one ever saw the Camp Director unless there was a problem. Cody and Joshua didn't have to guess that they were the problem.

"You two!" Mr. Henderson called to them as they arrived in main camp from their campsite trail. "In my office now!"

"Shit," Robby said. Robby had a nasty habit of getting frightened even though he wasn't in trouble himself.

"Maybe you can handle your father, but how about the Camp Director?" Nick asked.

"Can we help?" Timmy inquired.

"We'll be fine," Cody insisted. He looked to Joshua and repeated, "Just let me do the talking."

"The Camp Director is a real fucker," Robby quickly muttered, before Nick could cover up his mouth again.

"We'll meet you at breakfast," Joshua said. "This shouldn't take long. Cody's got everything worked out."

The group split up as Timmy, Robby, and Nick headed for the Dining Hall, and Cody and Joshua headed for the main office where the Camp Director waited for them.

171

"So what's the plan?" Josh asked with total confidence in his friend.

"Just let me do the talking," Cody said confidently.

"Fine, just tell me what you're going to say?"

"I haven't the slightest," Cody said.

"Fuck!" Joshua responded, instantly realizing that Robby's language skills were rubbing off on him.

When they arrived at the administrative building where the Camp Director's office was located, the office manager, Jack Riley, opened the door and motioned for the two boys to enter. Mr. Henderson himself hadn't arrived yet, and they could tell from Riley's tone that they were to remain silent until he had arrived. As Josh and Cody entered the office, they immediately noticed that they were not alone. Levi sat on a chair in front of Mr. Henderson's desk. He had an angry look on his face. It was no longer bleeding; the first aid nurse had seen to that.

"Nice improvement," Cody said, referring to Levi's face.

Levi was furious and jerked forward, like he was going to get up and attack.

Jack Riley displayed a killer expression, and Levi sat back down.

Josh and Cody sat down as well. Cody realized that this was going to be more difficult than he thought. Handling his father would be impossible enough, especially since the subject was homosexuality. But now somehow he had to deal with the Camp Director, his father, and Levi all at the same time.

Mr. Henderson walked in and slammed the door shut behind him.

"Do you know where I should be right now?!" he angrily asked the frightened boys.

CHAPTER TEN

"At breakfast!" he shouted, answering his own question. "Your Scoutmaster is on his way," he added, addressing all three boys at once. "I'm sure he'll have plenty to say when I'm finished with you." He paused before continuing. "We do not tolerate fighting at this camp! Now someone tell me what happened, and this better be good."

"The faggot started it!" Levi yelled, standing up and pointing furiously at Joshua.

"Silence!" Mr. Henderson shouted back to Levi. "You will be civil in this office." Levi sat back down.

The Camp Director then addressed Cody and Joshua. "Now, I don't know if the rumors about you two are correct or not," he said. "But if they are, I assure you there is no place for the two of you in Scouting. We don't tolerate that kind of perversion in this organization."

Just then, the door opened and Jim Meeder walked in. Only Cody and Joshua appreciated the irony. Behind Jim was a very angry looking Pastor Bob. Mr. Henderson had sent Jim to get him. He entrusted many tasks to Jim Meeder. Jim was mature and well-respected amongst the camp administrators and the Scoutmasters. He would be up for Camp Director himself in a year or two.

"Pastor Bob, thank you for coming," Mr. Henderson said.

Pastor Bob ignored him and looked straight at his son. "This better be damn good!" he shouted to Cody.

For a moment Mr. Henderson thought that Pastor Bob was going to hit Cody. But Pastor Bob got himself under control and sat down.

"Now, perhaps you can clarify a few things for us," Mr. Henderson said.

"That damn queer started it!" Pastor Bob shouted, echoing Levi's earlier remarks. Pastor Bob then looked to his son. "I thought I warned you to stay away from him!"

"He's a fag too!" Levi declared, pointing to Cody. "He told us all!"

Pastor Bob looked over to Levi angrily. "You better take that back." Before Levi could respond, Pastor Bob looked at Cody. "The next words out of your mouth better be 'it's not true,'" Pastor Bob warned his son.

Cody sat there quietly. Sweat began to form on his forehead. Everyone was looking at him, waiting for him to respond. Joshua was about to jump in, but he resisted. He remembered all of Cody's warnings. He had to have faith in him.

Cody took a deep breath and let it out. He was ready now. He had it all planned out. "Just be irrational," he thought to himself.

"Well Dad," he began confidently. "I had to help Joshua. I didn't want him to go to hell."

"Wait a minute" the Camp Director said confused. "Who's going to hell?"

"Joshua is!" Levi yelled.

"Dad said Joshua was going to hell for being gay," Cody regained control of the conversation. "So I decided to convince him to be straight again," Cody said innocently and with a surprisingly straight face.

"What the hell are you talking about, kid?" Mr. Henderson inquired. "What do you mean convince him?" the Camp Director asked.

"My father says people choose to be gay, to be attracted to other guys. So I decided to convince Joshua to choose to be attracted to women again." Cody paused for a moment, scanning everyone in the room for some sign that it was working. He continued, "Joshua is straight again."

Cody looked over to Joshua for support. "Right, Josh? Tell them."

Joshua looked surprised. There was no way in the world that they would buy this, he thought to himself.

"Um, yeah," he finally responded.

"That's the craziest thing I ever heard in my life," Mr. Henderson interrupted.

Cody saw that he wasn't buying it. He knew he had to do something.

"Dad?" Cody called. "Didn't you say people choose to be gay?" he asked innocently.

Pastor Bob was completely disarmed. Everyone in the room was staring at him. He didn't know how to answer. He couldn't deny it. All his beliefs concerning the sinful nature of homosexuality depended on it being a choice. If it wasn't a choice, then there was no conscious attempt to violate God's commandments. Cody had taken Pastor Bob's beliefs to their logical conclusion and used them against him.

"You can choose to be straight again, right Dad?"

"Uh, right, I guess. I never really thought about it that way," Pastor Bob said embarrassingly. He didn't know what else to say.

"Thank you, sir," Joshua said to Pastor Bob. "Now I won't go to hell."

Cody looked over to Joshua. "Shut up," he whispered, "let me do the talking."

"Well, uh, you're welcome kid," Pastor Bob replied awkwardly.

"I've never heard of anything like this," Mr. Henderson said unconvinced.

"That's because you're not a minister. My father knows everything," Cody said. "He can quote you any passage from the Bible, right Dad?"

Pastor Bob remained silent as he pondered the situation.

"This is bullshit!" Levi jumped in. "The faggot hit me!"

"Watch your language!" Pastor Bob yelled at Levi. "Haven't you been listening. He's not gay anymore." Pastor Bob could hardly believe what he had just said.

"Is it true? Did you hit Levi?" the Camp Director asked Joshua. He liked the topic of violence much better. Fighting was something he could understand. It was familiar territory.

Joshua didn't know what to say. Neither did Cody. Cody had been so busy concentrating on a way to get them off the hook for homosexuality that he completely forgot about the fight. Joshua could get sent home for that.

"No," Cody explained. "Levi attacked Joshua because he thought he was gay. He didn't believe that Joshua could choose to be straight again. He didn't believe my Dad."

Pastor Bob shot Levi an annoyed look.

"Perhaps my father needs to give Levi a few more sermons."

Joshua nodded in agreement.

"Well, this is a difficult situation. I can understand Levi's confusion," the Camp Director said. "Pastor Bob, feel free to deal with your Scouts as you please. Now let's get some breakfast." Mr. Henderson was relieved to dismiss the problem.

Joshua and Cody stood up and began to walk out the door. They could not believe they were getting away with this. Cody was right, Joshua realized, irrationality was the only way to handle his father.

CHAPTER 11

After the meeting with the Camp Director, Jim Meeder was instructed to bring both Cody and Levi back to their OA work projects. The two would be allowed to continue with their initiation, but one more offense would disqualify them permanently from the Order.

Levi and Cody followed close behind Jim Meeder as he escorted the two back. Cody sensed the rage and abhorrence radiating from Levi. But Levi remained silent. He could say nothing with Jim Meeder present and with Pastor Bob buying into their dubious defense.

"Keep these two separate for the rest of the day," Jim Meeder said to the OA taskmaster as he arrived at the ceremonial area. "If they talk at all, they are not allowed to continue," Jim commanded.

"Whatever," the taskmaster acknowledged. As Jim walked away, he turned and looked at Cody one last time. Jim nodded his head, silently communicating a "nice job" to Cody. Jim was on his side, Cody realized. The taskmaster then sent the two boys to opposite ends of the ceremonial area where the other candidates busily cleaned up brush.

As the two boys walked to their respective work projects, Levi looked back at Cody. "This is not over, you fucking queer," he whispered.

Levi's threat was inaudible to the taskmaster. But Cody heard it quite well. He knew Joshua would be facing similar problems throughout the day from Levi's gang, and Cody hoped he would be okay. At least, Cody thought, Joshua was no longer alone.

*****

Joshua left the Scoutmaster's office and waited at the benches for Robby, Timmy, and Nick to finish breakfast. He didn't have to wait long. The three left breakfast early since Pastor Bob wasn't around to stop them. Pastor Bob had gone straight back to the campsite following their meeting with the Camp Director. The entire conversation bewildered him, and he had a lot of thinking to do.

Joshua tensed up as his friends approached. He was more comfortable now that he knew they accepted him, but it was still difficult to discuss the subject, and he knew his friends would have lots of questions.

"So what happened?" Nick and Tim asked simultaneously.

"Did he kill you?" Robby asked.

"Do I look dead?" Joshua responded.

"You mean, Pastor Brimstone Bob doesn't care if you're gay?" Nick asked unconvinced.

"I'm not gay anymore," Joshua said, as if his excuse made perfect sense.

"What?" they all asked simultaneously. Confusion was becoming the norm lately.

Joshua dutifully explained, "Cody decided that if his father believes people choose to be gay, then they could also choose to be straight. So, I chose to be attracted to women right in front of Pastor Bob. So, now I'm either normal, or Pastor Bob has to face the fact that the Bible which he spent his life studying has some major holes in it." Joshua was starting to enjoy this.

"That's the craziest thing I ever heard," Timmy said.

Robby nodded in agreement.

"We finally got used to the fact that you liked guys, and now you are saying you like girls?" Timmy said confused.

"I'll never understand religion," Nick added.

"Well, since you like girls now, how about that First Aid nurse?" Nick teased.

"Too soon," Robby jumped in.

Joshua laughed. He was relieved by the way his friends had come around. It still hurt that they had remained silent when he needed help, but he now knew it was out of fear and not malice. Besides, they were trying desperately to make up for it.

"What about Levi's pack?" Timmy asked.

"Yeah," Nick agreed. "Not everyone is as insane as Pastor Bob. They won't buy into this whole choice thing."

"I don't know," Josh replied. "I don't know what I'm going to do."

"What we are going to do," Robby corrected.

Joshua was glad to hear Robby say that. Robby had taken the whole situation worse than anyone. He wanted to defend Joshua from the beginning, but he was afraid to speak. He felt horrible knowing that he had betrayed the one guy who had stood up for him. But now Robby seemed determined to defend his friend to the very end.

The friends decided it would be best to avoid main camp for the rest of the day. The less contact they had with Levi's gang, the better. For the most part this wouldn't be a problem. They could skip their merit badges, they reasoned. These sessions were always light on content on Thursday since so many people had been inducted into the OA. The boys would have to return only for lunch and dinner, and they felt they could slip in and out of meals without incident. Then they would all meet up with Cody after dinner when he finished his induction. Safety in numbers, that was the plan. All they had to do was stay together.

*****

Joshua and his friends had a lot of time to kill before they would be reunited with Cody after dinner. They needed to find a nice secluded spot, someplace where they wouldn't run into Levi's gang, Pastor Bob, or anyone else. With over 300 campers present, this proved difficult.

"Obviously our campsite is out of the question," reasoned Joshua. "People are going in and out of there all day."

"How about the lakefront?" Timmy offered.

"No, that's always crowded," he said, rejecting his own proposal.

"Maybe the Desert?" he suggested, trying again.

"Too hot there," he realized, once again rejecting his own plan.

"How about the archives?" Nick chimed in.

"The what?" inquired Timmy, beating Josh and Robby to the same question.

"The camp archives," Nick repeated. Nick had been coming to camp the longest, so he knew about things that no one else had ever heard of.

"It's where they store a bunch of camp memorabilia," he continued. "You know, old pictures and patches and stuff, that sort of thing?"

He continued, "Anyway, a few years back someone got the idea to display the stuff in a small room in the administrative building. They only open it twice a week because no one really ever goes in there." He paused and then qualified himself, "Well, except for some of the old Scoutmasters."

"That's perfect!" Joshua said, "Ken Fenton wouldn't be caught dead near the archives." Or anyone else for that matter, Joshua figured.

Joshua led the way as the group briskly headed towards the archives. Robby struggled to keep up with Joshua's pace, determined not to let Joshua out of his sight. Never again would he let Joshua believe he was alone.

*****

Very few people were in the administrative building at this time of day. Occasionally, one might spot the Camp Director in his office, but more often that not he was out talking with the Scoutmasters. An intermittent Scoutmaster might pop into the building to take advantage of the free coffee offered to all Scoutmasters, but this rarely happened so soon after breakfast. The only person staffing the administrative building was the office manager, Jack Riley. He often went unseen, having to staff the offices all day. He spent most of his time doing paper work, answering phone calls, and most importantly, keeping Scoutmasters happy. This later task mostly consisted of keeping the coffee pot filled. Jack was the first line of defense for any Scoutmaster coming to complain to the Camp Director. He realized a long time ago that the smell of coffee diffused most Scoutmasters and made them more manageable.

Jack was surprised when the four boys walked in the door. He was used to seeing only adults in the building. Jack, of course, stopped them immediately.

"The bathroom is for Scoutmasters only," Jack said angrily. "You'll have to use the outhouses at your campsite." This was Jack's token response to the occasional younger Scout who sauntered into the building to take advantage of the clean flush toilets available only to adult leaders and counselors.

"We came to look at the archives," Nick said politely.

"What?" Jack asked surprised.

"The place where you keep all the old camp stuff," Nick explained.

Jack looked angry. "I know what they are, I was just surprised you wanted to see them." So few people came around to see them that Jack hadn't even bothered to unlock the room.

"What do you want to see them for anyway?" he inquired.

"We are working on History merit badge," Nick quickly responded.

"Oh," said Jack, "Just a minute, I'll get the keys." Jack picked up the keys and brought the boys down into the basement. He unlocked the door to the archives and told the boys that they could take all the time they wanted.

"I didn't know there was a History merit badge," Timmy said to Nick after Jack left the room.

"There isn't," he responded. For a moment, they all had a new appreciation for Nick.

The room was small, seemingly more like a big walk-in closet than a display area. The displays consisted mostly of open boxes with writing on the side indicating its contents. One box was simply marked, "Old Patches." Nick and Timmy scampered through them. The collection included camp patches going back to the 1950s. The camp had issued new patches every year, with different designs on them, to the eager few who collected them. As Timmy and Nick looked through them, something caught Joshua's eye from across the room. He saw a box marked, "Troop Pictures." Joshua slowly walked over to the box. He seemed lost in thought. Robby shadowed him closely.

Joshua opened the box and started looking through the pictures. The box held a collection of photos of the different troops and Scouters who attended the camp every summer. Mr. Henderson went around to each campsite during the week to snap a troop photo. He gave one copy to each Scoutmaster at the end of the week, and another copy made its way into the archives. The photos were organized in folders designated by year. Joshua carefully sifted through each folder.

Robby didn't understand why Joshua was so interested in these pictures all of a sudden. Josh did not just casually glance at them; he seemed to be looking for someone in particular. Robby thought that perhaps Joshua had an older brother or other relative that had gone to camp before.

"Who are you looking for?" Robby finally questioned.

"No one," Josh said quickly, not wanting Robby's question to distract him.

"Joshua put down the folder for 1955 and went to 1954, repeating his scans. When he finished with 1950, there were no more folders left. But there were still a bunch of loose pictures in the box underneath the folders. Apparently, those photos had never been cataloged. Perhaps no one knew what year they were taken?

Joshua gently picked up a group of black and white photos that seemed really old. He wasn't sure how far back they went, but the uniforms looked like they were from the thirties or forties, Joshua guessed. One picture sort of jumped out at him. A troop number on one of the Scout uniforms in the photo caught his eye. It was Troop 24, his troops' number. Joshua didn't realize that Troop 24 went back that far. Evidently Pastor Bob was not the first Scoutmaster for their troop.

Robby wandered back over to Timmy and Nick. They had discovered a box of old Scout uniforms and were trying them on. They laughed at the poor fashion statements made by these earlier Scouts. Robby found an old beret and had to wear it. The three boys giggled as Robby flaunted his new hat. The fun was short-lived. Joshua jumped back in astonishment, letting out a barely audible cry. The boys stopped their fashion show and immediately looked to Joshua.

Joshua stood still holding one of the photos with his mouth agape. He had a cold, blank stare as he gazed at the picture. His hands slightly trembled.

"What's wrong?" Robby asked concerned, as he ran over to Josh. The others quickly followed.

Joshua said nothing. He just pointed to the face of a boy in the picture. The boy had blond hair and a frail body. He stood off to the side of the troop picture, seemingly isolated from the rest of the boys, even though he was part of the troop picture. He was the only boy in the picture who wasn't smiling. Rather, his face held a sad, lonely expression.

"Wow!" Nick uttered excitedly, as he gazed at the photo. "It looks just like you," he said looking at Robby.

"Wow, it does!" Timmy agreed.

"No it doesn't," Robby opposed.

"No," Joshua finally spoke. He instantly recognized the identity of the kid, even though he had never seen him before in real life. The face resembled exactly the boy he had been dreaming about all week.

"It's Tommy Drapos," Joshua said quietly.

"Who?" inquired Timmy.

"Tommy Drapos."

"How do you know?"

"I just do," Joshua said, still gazing at the picture. "I just do."

The boys were silent as a chill gripped each of them. Robby eyed the photo carefully trying to understand why Timmy and Nick thought the boy looked like him. Personally, he thought the boy in the picture looked like Joshua.

*****

Cody worked long and hard all day and it took its toll. But his exhaustion was mental as much as it was physical. Late in the afternoon, the taskmasters ended the work projects and brought the OA candidates over to the showers to wash off from the long day's work. Cody needed the reprieve. Soon afterwards, they were taken back to the ceremonial area where the taskmasters presented them with their first full meal of the day. The candidates gulped down their food as though they hadn't eaten in years. After dinner, the ordeal was over for them, and the candidates could now rejoin the rest of the camp. Most importantly, they could talk again.

Cody had forgotten about Levi's earlier threat. The two worked apart from each other all day, and the hard labor gave Cody something else on which to focus. Vengeance, however, eternally occupied Levi's mind. Soon after the initiation ended, Levi made his move.

He needed to catch Cody before he made it back too far into main camp. Cody walked quietly, oblivious to his stalker. Levi smashed into him from behind, knocking him to the rough ground.

"Excuse me," Levi said, "they shouldn't let girls on the trail." Levi kicked Cody hard in the stomach. "They could get hurt." He followed the kick with a gob of saliva, which he furiously and expertly delivered directly onto Cody's face.

Robby, Timmy, Nick, and Joshua witnessed the entire incident. They had been waiting for Cody at main camp, knowing the initiation ended after dinner. Joshua saw Levi knock Cody to the ground. Levi went in for another kick, but instantly took notice of the onlookers. He saw Josh and froze. Like an angry bull, Josh charged.

Levi fled instantly into the woods, and Josh returned to his friend. Levi knew he wasn't prepared to take Joshua on, especially with all of his friends around. He didn't like those odds.

Joshua reached Cody and helped him up. "Are you okay?" he asked.

"I'm fine," Cody responded, dismissing Josh's concern. "But Levi is not going to let this rest."

The other three boys caught up to Josh and Cody.

"Levi backed down way too easily," Cody said to Joshua. "Something is definitely up." The boys agreed.

CHAPTER ELEVEN

*****

Dark clouds covered a portion of the early evening sky, but no one had noticed them moving in. The sun still remained uncovered, and in the forest no one really noticed clouds in the distant until they darkened the sun. Thunder was a different story altogether. A discerning listener could fathom a storm coming hours prior to its arrival just by listening for the thunder in the distance. But this storm brewed silently, like a predator stalking its prey.

Cody was thankful to be reunited with his friends again after the long, hard day of work. He was especially glad to be with Joshua again. The group had millions of questions for Cody about the OA, but Cody wasn't allowed to discuss it. OA members were not supposed to ruin the experience for future members.

But the experience hadn't really meant that much for Cody. The OA was created to recognize those who best exemplified what Scouting stood for. If someone like Levi could become a member, Cody felt, then Scouting didn't stand for much of anything. As far as Cody was concerned, the past day had been a waste of his time. The moments spent with his friends were infinitely more valuable.

"Were you scared being by yourself last night?" Nick asked.

"What were the secret ceremonies like?" Timmy jumped in.

"Do the hot coals hurt your feet?" Robby asked concerned. Everyone pondered Robby's question. Robby had heard many rumors about the OA initiations, but the dreaded hot coal walking ceremony was foremost amongst them. Cody couldn't believe some of the stuff the first year Scouts spread.

"No," Cody finally replied, "If you cover your feet with mud first, it doesn't hurt that much." Cody held back a smile. Robby seemed to contemplate this. The others caught onto the joke right away.

The boys finally broke out in laughter, bringing Robby in on the joke. Joshua didn't laugh, however. He had remained curiously silent since he had seen the image of Tommy Drapos on that photo.

Ken Fenton had been following the group since dinner. He had made his way to the entrance of the Tommy Drapos Trail. The heavy concentration of shrubs at the trail's opening conveniently concealed him from view.

"What's wrong, Red Feather?" Cody finally asked Joshua, concerned about his silence. For a moment Cody wondered if Joshua was still mad at him.

"I have to be alone for a little while," Josh replied, without an explanation.

"Why?" Cody inquired.

"There is something I have to do?" he reluctantly responded.

"I'll go with you," Cody insisted.

Cody followed Joshua who had already started down the Tommy Drapos trail. Nick placed his arm on Cody's shoulder to hold him back. "That's fine," Nick called to Joshua. "We'll meet you at the beach."

"No," added Robby, "We'll wait for you right here."

After Joshua was out of hearing range, Cody wanted some answers.

"What's going on? What's wrong with Red Feather?"

"It's something about Tommy Drapos," Nick answered. "He's been like this since he found the picture of Tommy in the archives this afternoon."

CHAPTER ELEVEN

"He found a picture of Tommy!" Cody spoke excitedly. "I thought he was a myth?" Cody questioned.

"Joshua doesn't think so," Nick said. "He is taking this whole thing very seriously."

Cody and the boys didn't really understand what was going through Joshua's mind, but they understood he had to be alone right now. They didn't have to understand Josh to support him. They were determined to wait for him at the trail entrance. The boys wanted there to be no chance that Levi and his gang would follow him down the trail and catch him alone. They watched Joshua disappear on the trail.

Ken darted through the forest, avoiding the trail, rushing hurriedly back towards the Trading Post. Levi's gang patiently awaited the results of Ken's intelligence gathering mission.

*****

The first noticeable flash of lightning from the approaching storm lit up the sky in a brilliant explosion of electrical discharge. The thunderous effect resonated with a deafening eruption. But the boys in Levi's gang were still able to distinguish the sound of Levi's angry voice as he approached.

"So, what did you do to the faggot while I was away?" Levi demanded, as he furiously advanced towards his gang, who were lollygagging behind the Trading Post.

"Hey, Levi! Congratulations on passing the ordeal!" offered one of the pack.

"Yeah, glad to have you back," said another.

"Cut the crap! I asked a question!" Levi wasn't in the mood for social graces. His mind was on one thing only.

"Well, nothing," his gang had to admit, knowing full well they were in trouble.

"We couldn't do anything," one member quickly explained, hoping to diffuse Levi's anger. "We looked for them all day, but we couldn't find them."

"Yeah, we covered the entire camp, and couldn't find them," another boy repeated.

It was a disingenuous excuse. They had looked for Joshua and his friends, but they had no idea what they were going to do if they actually found them. They had no plan.

"Can't you guys do anything without me?" Levi interrupted angrily.

"Chill Levi," said one of the boys confidently. "We did send Ken to follow them after dinner." Ken felt honored as though he was singled out for an important mission. Mostly, though, the boys just wanted to get rid of him. No one expected him to uncover anything useful.

The cracking of sticks betrayed Ken's presence closing in on the gang from the woods.

"Who's there?" Levi demanded, looking towards the noise.

"Relax, it's just Ken. He must have some info," one of the boys said.

"It's me," Ken whispered from the woods.

"See, we're not completely incompetent," defended one of the boys.

Levi ignored him.

Ken's legs were scratched up a bit from his trek through the woods, and he was breathing heavily.

"It's perfect," Ken explained between breaths, as he approached them. He wiped some dirt off of his uniform before continuing. "Joshua is all alone now."

CHAPTER ELEVEN

"Where?!" Levi demanded.

"Follow me," Ken offered, pleased at the attention.

Ken turned around and headed back into the woods towards the Tommy Drapos Trail. Levi and his friends followed right behind him. Several more flashes of lightening illuminated the sky. It was going to be quite a storm.

CHAPTER 12

Nick had been coming to camp for five years now. He knew storms came up quickly, and he always kept a pocket poncho on him. After a few more flashes of lightening, he opened up his belt-pack and unraveled the poncho.

"Good planning," Timmy said, observing Nick.

"Be prepared," Nick said back.

The boys sat at the entrance to the Tommy Drapos trail, anxiously awaiting the return of their friend. They didn't know where Joshua went or why he had gone. They weren't even sure how long he would be gone. All they knew is that it was going to start pouring down rain any second now. The rain didn't matter to any of them. Robby especially had already made up his mind that no matter how bad the storm got, he would wait all night for Joshua if he had to.

"Looks awfully hot under that poncho," Timmy said to Nick. "As your friend, I'm obliged to offer to wear it for you."

"No," Cody jumped in, "allow me to bear your burden."

Nick laughed. "Don't worry about me," he said, "the hot temperature will be nice once the cold rain starts drenching everything."

Timmy tried another tactic. "You realize, of course, that when it starts to rain, there are three of us against one of you."

192

Nick wasn't sure he liked the sound of that. His three friends stared at him intently. Nick dropped his smile. "You wouldn't," Nick said.

The boys pounced on him. Timmy and Cody got to him first, while Robby snuck up from behind. The tickling commenced. Nick rolled to the ground laughing ferociously as the three boys concentrated their attack on his stomach.

The sky opened up in a downpour, immediately drenching all of them and breaking up their game. The boys huddled together and wrapped themselves with Nick's poncho.

"Assholes," Nick said to his friends, as he squeezed close to them under his poncho.

Cody was the first to notice Jim Meeder frantically running towards them. He was drenched, and his feet were encased in mud. He was in a panic.

"Get back to the Dining Hall immediately!" he shouted, as he approached the boys. "I just heard it on the radio! This whole area is under a tornado watch."

He continued, "I'm heading to the administrative building to sound the camp alarm." The camp siren was loud enough to be heard at each of the campsites. When signaled, the Scouts all knew they were to congregate at the Dining Hall.

"We're waiting for Joshua," Robby shouted, unsure if anyone could hear him over the sound of the rain impacting the ground.

"He's on the trail!" Timmy informed Jim, "and he'll be right back."

"No," Jim shouted in response, "You have to get to the Dining Hall. It is too dangerous to wait! After I sound the siren, I'll go after him!"

The boys followed Jim as he ran towards the administrative building, intent on making sure he lived up to his promise after sounding the alarm. As they ran toward the administrative building, they saw that the Dining Hall was already filling up with people. Most Scouts didn't need a siren to tell them that the Dining Hall was the driest place in camp right now.

Jim Meeder frantically fingered through his pockets looking for the keys to the office. He quickly found them and opened the door. Before he could remove his keys from the lock, the boys had already piled in. Only then did they all notice that someone was missing.

"Hey!" Cody cried out. Their shouts were much more apparent now that they were inside away from the noisy deluge. "Where's Robby!" No one answered. They all realized where Robby had gone.

*****

Joshua had reached Tommy's Point right before the sky opened up. The sky was dark and menacing, and thunder reverberated throughout the forest. The Point held a new significance for Joshua. The images from his dreams merged with the real world. Tommy Drapos was a factual person, and Joshua now knew exactly what he looked like. Tommy lived once in flesh and blood. He roamed these campgrounds, and interacted with real people at this very camp decades prior. And right at this exact spot, Joshua realized, the Demon had extinguished the innocent, lonely boy's life.

Joshua took the troop picture out from where he had concealed it underneath his shirt. Rainwater immediately drenched it. He gazed at Tommy once again and began to cry.

CHAPTER TWELVE

"I wish I could have helped you," he said softly, as his voice cracked. Tears began to cover the picture.

Josh laid the photo aside and began to dig a small hole with his hands. Shoveling like a dog, he burrowed a foot-deep hole and placed the picture of Tommy Drapos in it. He carefully covered up the picture with mud and laid some wildflowers over it. He knelt over the grave on his knees and bowed his head in prayer.

"Great Spirit," Joshua prayed softly and reverently, not really believing god was listening. He paused for a second in thought before continuing. "Please watch over Tommy Drapos. Let him rest and be happy."

Joshua paused again. He hadn't thought this prayer out ahead of time, and now he didn't know what to say for Tommy. He just sensed that he had to do something. The image of Tommy Drapos' broken body once again invaded his thoughts. Anger quickly eclipsed his solemn tone.

"God, why didn't you help him!" Joshua raged. A thunderous blast shot across the sky. Joshua was drenched. He took his shirt off but couldn't tell the difference. He was freezing, but it didn't matter to him. He came and did what he had intended to do, what someone should have done a long time ago. He took one more glance at Tommy Drapos' fresh grave, then he turned around and headed down the trail back towards camp.

*****

Joshua raced down the Tommy Drapos trail desperately trying not to slip. The trail had become a waterslide, as it often did

195

during a severe storm. Joshua's mind had been so intent on laying Tommy to rest that he failed to notice how severe the weather had become. Now, he could not help but notice. Even at his distance from camp, Joshua could hear the emergency siren sounding in the background.

The trail was winding and exceedingly slippery from the mud formed since the downpour. Joshua gave full attention to navigating the twists and turns of the slippery trail at the maximum safe speed possible. He failed to notice the dark silhouettes on the trail up ahead that were approaching him fast, and then it was too late. Joshua stopped just before colliding with the darkness. Only then did a brilliant flash of lightning reveal his visitors.

"Where are you going, faggot?" Levi asked, standing before Joshua only inches away from him. His gang members stood silently behind him.

"Let me through!" Josh threatened, holding his ground.

Two of the gang members positioned themselves behind Joshua. They grabbed his arms from behind and held him tight. Even so, they had trouble keeping him still as Joshua struggled to break free.

Levi removed his own shirt, revealing a black handle stuck in his pants. He clenched it tightly, and pulled out the long, sharp knife. Pocket knives were quite common at camp. Hunting knives, however, were strictly forbidden. Even Levi's gang seemed caught off guard by this maneuver.

"Jesus Christ, Levi! Are you crazy?" Ken Fenton frantically asked, as he stood behind Levi astonished. Levi didn't answer. He just gazed furiously into Joshua's eyes. His expression revealed an unquenchable abhorrence.

CHAPTER TWELVE

"I would stop struggling if I were you, or you might get seriously hurt." Levi's stare indicated a threat, not a statement of concern.

Joshua instantly ceased his attempt to break free as he noticed the knife in Levi's hands. He knew Levi was fully capable of hurting others, but he only now understood how far Levi could go.

"Help them," Levi commanded three of his pack, who were still standing behind him. The boys quickly joined their friends in restraining Joshua.

Joshua was afraid. Bullies didn't bother Josh. He knew how to stand up to them. But Joshua had never experienced anything like this.

"What are you going to do?" Joshua sobbed, desperately trying to disguise his fear.

"Shut up, faggot!" Levi screamed. He paused for a second to collect himself. His expression transformed into a smile, but fury and loathing still protruded from his eyes.

"You have nothing to fear," he informed Joshua. "We are just going to give you what every faggot wants."

Levi motioned to his friends. "Do it!" he commanded.

They grabbed at Joshua's belt, quickly unbuckling it, while three other boys yanked down his pants. Joshua stood there in his boxers, cold and frightened.

A brilliant luminescent flash of lightening ripped through the sky, followed almost immediately by another. A fierce darkness separated the two flashes.

In that instant, Joshua recalled the lucidity of his nightmare. He saw the bullies from his vision cornering and raping Tommy Drapos with sticks. He saw Tommy's naked body cower before them as he screamed in pain. Another burst of lightening awakened Joshua from his flashback.

Levi pointed to a long, thick stick lying on the ground near Joshua and motioned for Ken to pick it up. Some of the boys began to laugh as they realized what Levi intended to do. Ken bent down to reach for the stick, still attempting to hold Josh with one hand. His balance was off.

Joshua knew what they were going to do. He had already seen it happen to Tommy Drapos. He also saw how it all ended. A burst of hate blasted through his psyche, completely dissipating any fear. The image of Tommy Drapos's dead body possessed him, and Joshua immediately took advantage of Ken's imbalance. As Ken bent down to reach for the stick, Joshua yanked his own arm forward, snapping Ken's grip and throwing him wildly off-balance.

Ken struggled to regain his poise, while Joshua sprung his free elbow back like a steel pipe, impacting Ken in the nose. Ken stumbled back in pain and fell to the mud. Blood poured from his nose and saturated his face. Before the others could react, Joshua tensed his other arm, locking two other gang members in a hold. He swiveled around quickly, dragging the boys with him. He tactically placed his right leg forward, completing the move. The two boys tripped on Joshua's leg and joined Ken in the mud. Joshua then burst through the other gang members before they could reclaim their hold. He ran fiercely back towards Tommy's Point.

"Get him!" Levi roared. But Levi no longer waited for anyone to follow through on his commands. He had already lunged ahead in pursuit of his target.

As Joshua fled down the trail towards Tommy's Point, flashbacks from his dream battered his thoughts. The scene of

Tommy running through the forest blended with his own predicament. At times, he couldn't distinguish the two separate worlds. Dream had become reality, and reality had become a nightmare. Lightening flashes relentlessly pounded the darkness, creating the illusion of a sunlit day. The Devil closed fast on Joshua. He could hear its laughter and its taunts. "You can't run, faggot!" it shouted over and over. "You can't hide!"

Joshua reached the grave he had dug at Tommy's Point and stopped before crashing into it. There was nowhere left to run. Tommy's Point was the end of the trail. He stood at the edge of the cliff and frantically turned around just in time to feel the Demon collide with him. Joshua struggled to get onto his feet again, but the slippery mud made that task impossible. Levi wrestled Joshua back to the ground, and Joshua fell on his back. Levi used his knees to pin Joshua on each side, trapping him from escape.

Joshua saw the face of the Demon looking down at him with fierce disgust. It was no dream, Joshua realized. The Demon was real, and it had Joshua trapped. There was nothing he could do.

"Die you faggot!" Levi screamed, as he raised the knife over his head. The other gang members arrived at Tommy's Point completely out of breath. They were stunned as they saw Levi raise the knife into the air, but they did nothing to stop him.

None of the gang saw Robby rush past them towards Levi. Robby saw Joshua's body lying helplessly on the ground, and he charged hysterically forward towards Josh's captor. The mud was wet and slippery, so Robby couldn't slow down even if he wanted to. He dove forward and plowed into Levi, knocking the knife from his hands. The force of the impact knocked Levi off balance, and he fell sideways next to the cliff. The inertia from the impact had ceased, but gravity took over. Water and mud rushed down the side of the cliff, and Levi desperately clutched the cliff-side to prevent himself from going with it.

Joshua caught a glance from Levi's eyes and watched them turn from hate to terror. Robby picked himself up and noticed what was happening. He desperately grabbed forward for Levi's hands, but it was too late. The Demon's desperate last words, a pitiful cry for help, could not break the deafening roar of thunder.

Suddenly, the sky went dark. It seemed like minutes before another flash revealed Levi's mangled and limp body on the rocks below. The nightmare was over, the Demon was dead.

Tears poured from Robby's eyes as he realized what had happened. His chest muscles tightened, strangling him as he grasped for air. He sounded like an asthmatic desperately gasping for life. Joshua grabbed him and hugged him tight.

Levi's gang could barely fathom what had happened. They gazed over the cliff unable to accept what they had witnessed. To them, it seemed like a dream. To Joshua, the dream had finally ended.

EPILOGUE

It was a beautiful summer evening, around 9:00 p.m. The last of the campers had entered the campfire area and seated themselves around the loud, crackling fire. Hundreds of Scouts eagerly awaited this official beginning to their first day of summer camp.

As Camp Director, Jim Meeder was obliged to begin the campfire program. He immensely enjoyed this part of the job. He got up after the last Scout troop was seated, and he solemnly walked over to the campfire. He stood quietly and respectfully in front of it. As the last camper quieted down, he spoke.

"I would like to welcome you all to the first week of summer camp. Our staff are skilled and talented, and they are here for you." Jim emphasized that point. "I hope you will take advantage of what the staff have to offer. With their help and your enthusiasm, we can make this the best week of the summer camp ever."

The crowd erupted with applause. It was an easy score.

Jim Meeder put his hand up in the air and gave the Scout Sign, consisting of four fingers pointing up, and the last pointed down. When this sign was given at any function, the crowd knew it was time to listen with respect. They settled down once again.

Jim continued his speech to the attentive crowd. "I would like to begin tonight's campfire with a story. This story is a camp legend which has been told here at each campfire for over 50 years now. The story is true, and I urge you to listen to it quietly and respectfully."

Jim paused for a moment and motioned over to Joshua who was sitting in the audience. He was 19-years-old now, and this was his second year on camp staff. Jim was pleased to have Josh as director of the Ecology area. His skills and knowledge aside, Josh showed respect and kindness to every Scout. This made him a natural teacher.

"Our nature director, Red Feather, will now deliver the camp legend," Jim announced, introducing Joshua to the crowd.

Joshua got up and walked over to the campfire. Applause rang out. Joshua was one of the most popular counselors. Cody and Robby celebrated the loudest, as they sat with the other camp staff members. They were proud to be on staff with Joshua.

Joshua stood silently and looked over the crowd intently. He recalled the first time he sat in the audience and heard the legend for the first time. How could he forget that terrible week? A boy died back then, but the tragedy went beyond one boy's death. In a sense, Robby died that night as well. Robby had undergone lots of counseling following the incident, and all of Robby's friends convinced him that Levi's death was unavoidable. But Robby was still never quite the same person. Those who had never known Robby prior to the incident noticed nothing wrong with him. But, Joshua and Cody detected it. They remembered the shy boy, scared of his own shadow, who shined brilliantly after discovering the security of friendship. Josh recalled Robby's little quirks, especially his knack for impressions, and, of course, his photographic memory for songs he had never heard. Robby didn't do impressions anymore, and he didn't recite songs. Many of those quirks died the day the demon fell from the cliff. Part of Robby, it seemed, died on that day as well.

But there would be no more victims. For two years now, Joshua was charged with telling the legend. As long as Joshua owned the story, he owned the power of the Demon.

"I want to tell you the story of a quiet, lonely boy named Tommy Drapos," Joshua said to the crowd. A tear formed in Robby's eye. Joshua also showed tears occasionally while telling the story. Some of the Scoutmasters would sometimes congratulate Josh on his effective performance after the campfire. But, Joshua wasn't performing.

Josh continued with the story. He told of the lonely boy with no friends. He told of how Tommy Drapos had wandered off by himself into the forest. He told of the Demon who stalked isolated kids and threw them off Tommy's Point. He warned everyone not to hike alone at night and to stay away from Tommy's Point.

"I thought the Beast only killed faggots!" a 12-year-old Scout from the audience yelled.

Many of the Scouters in the audience began to laugh, including a few of the Scoutmasters. Joshua remembered when he had heard that for the first time himself.

Joshua walked over to the boy who made the comment and looked deep into his eyes. The camper noticed an intense pain and rage in Joshua's eyes, and the boy's smile evaporated.

"I have seen the Demon kill," he yelled. "It does not discriminate!" Joshua gazed at the audience. "No one is free from its hatred. As long as it exists, everyone is a victim." He looked again into the boy's eyes. "You are all Tommy Drapos."

Joshua spoke from experience. He had seen the Demon in his dreams and in real life. In fact, he had seen it many times since that night. He saw it at home, at church, on TV. He even saw it right before him at that very moment in the form of a 12-year-old boy looking for attention. Joshua knew more than anyone that the Demon had victims far beyond its intended target.

But the Demon would not kill this week, Joshua knew, not as long as he was on staff and as long as people recognized the Demon for what it truly was. Joshua had seen the Devil's face and recognized it. Now he was going to describe the Demon to the entire audience, so they would recognize it too. That, Joshua finally understood, was how you defeat the Devil.

About the Author

Jay Jordan Hawke is a former Eagle Scout and Boy Scout camp counselor. He holds a Ph.D. in History. He currently lives in the Midwest, and he deeply misses his friends on the Lac Du Flambeau Ojibwa reservation in northern Wisconsin. This is his first novel. Visit Jay Hawke on the web and leave feedback at: http://www.jayhawke.weebly.com